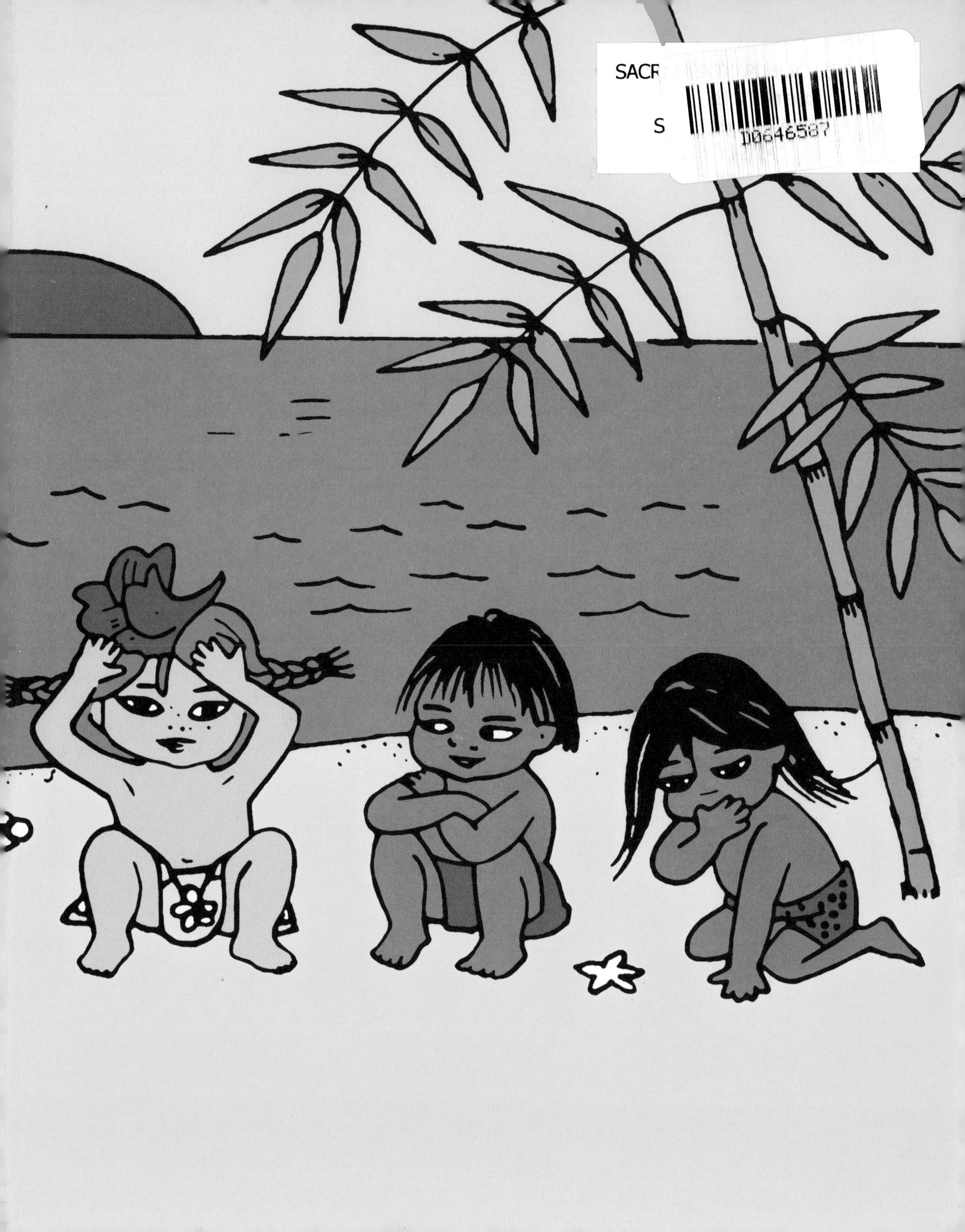

Text is © 1957, 1958, 1959, & 2014 by Astrid Lindgren, Saltkråkan AB. Illustrations are © 1957, 1958, 1959, & 2014 by Ingrid Vang Nyman, Saltkråkan AB. English translation is © 2014 by Tiina Nunnally. Illustrations are revised, restored, and colored by Björn Hedlund. Published by agreement with Rabén & Sjögren Agency. All rights reserved. No part of this book (except small portions for review purposes) may be reproduced in any form without written permission from Enfant or Rabén & Sjögren. Enfant is an imprint of Drawn & Quarterly. Originally published as *Pippi Vill Inte Bli Stor Och Andra Serier* in 2011 by Rabén & Sjögren (ISBN 978-91-29-67607-5). The translation of this book was funded by the Swedish Arts Council. *drawnandquarterly.com*. First hardcover edition: November 2014. Printed in China. 10 9 8 7 6 5 4 3 2 1. Library and Archives Canada Cataloguing in Publication: Lindgren, Astrid, 1907–2002 [*Pippi Vill Inte Bli Stor Och Andra Serier*. English]. *Pippi Won't Grow Up* / by Astrid Lindgren and Ingrid Vang Nyman; translated by Tiina Nunnally. Translation of: *Pippi Vill Inte Bli Stor Och Andra Serier*. ISBN 978-1-77046-168-0 (pbk.) 1. Graphic novels. I. Vang-Nyman, Ingrid, 1916–1959, artist II. Nunnally, Tiina, 1952–, translator III. Title. IV. Title: *Pippi Vill Inte Bli Stor Och Andra Serier*. English. PZ7.7.L55Piv 2014 j741.5'9485 C2013-908540-8. Distributed in the USA by Farrar, Straus and Giroux; Orders: 888.330.8477. Distributed in Canada by Raincoast Books; Orders: 800.663.5714. Distributed in the United Kingdom by Publishers Group UK; Orders: info@pguk.co.uk.

Astrid Lindgren's

Pippi

Won't Grow Up

By Astrid Lindgren &
Ingrid Vang Nyman

Translated by Tiina Nunnally

ENFANT

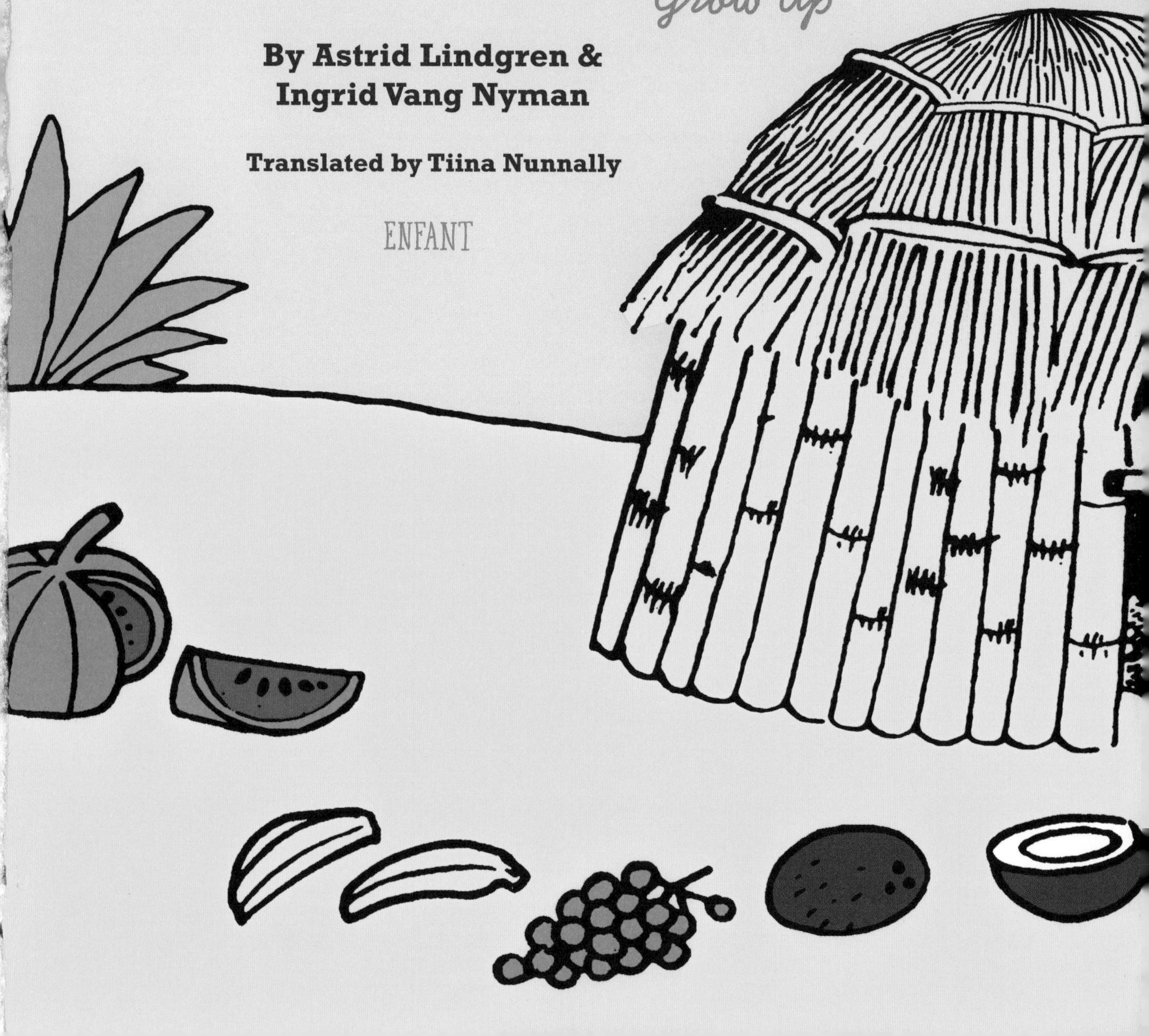

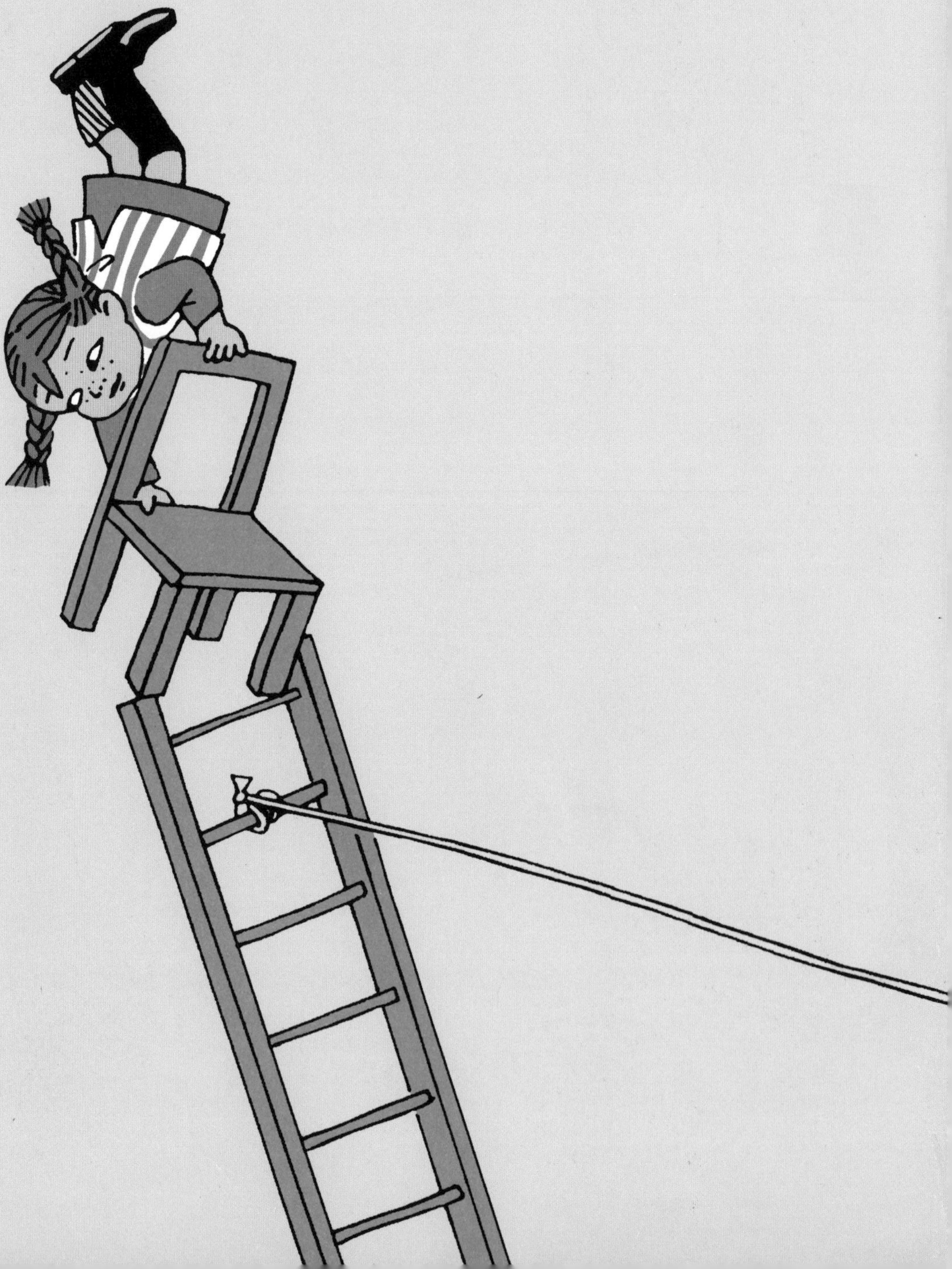

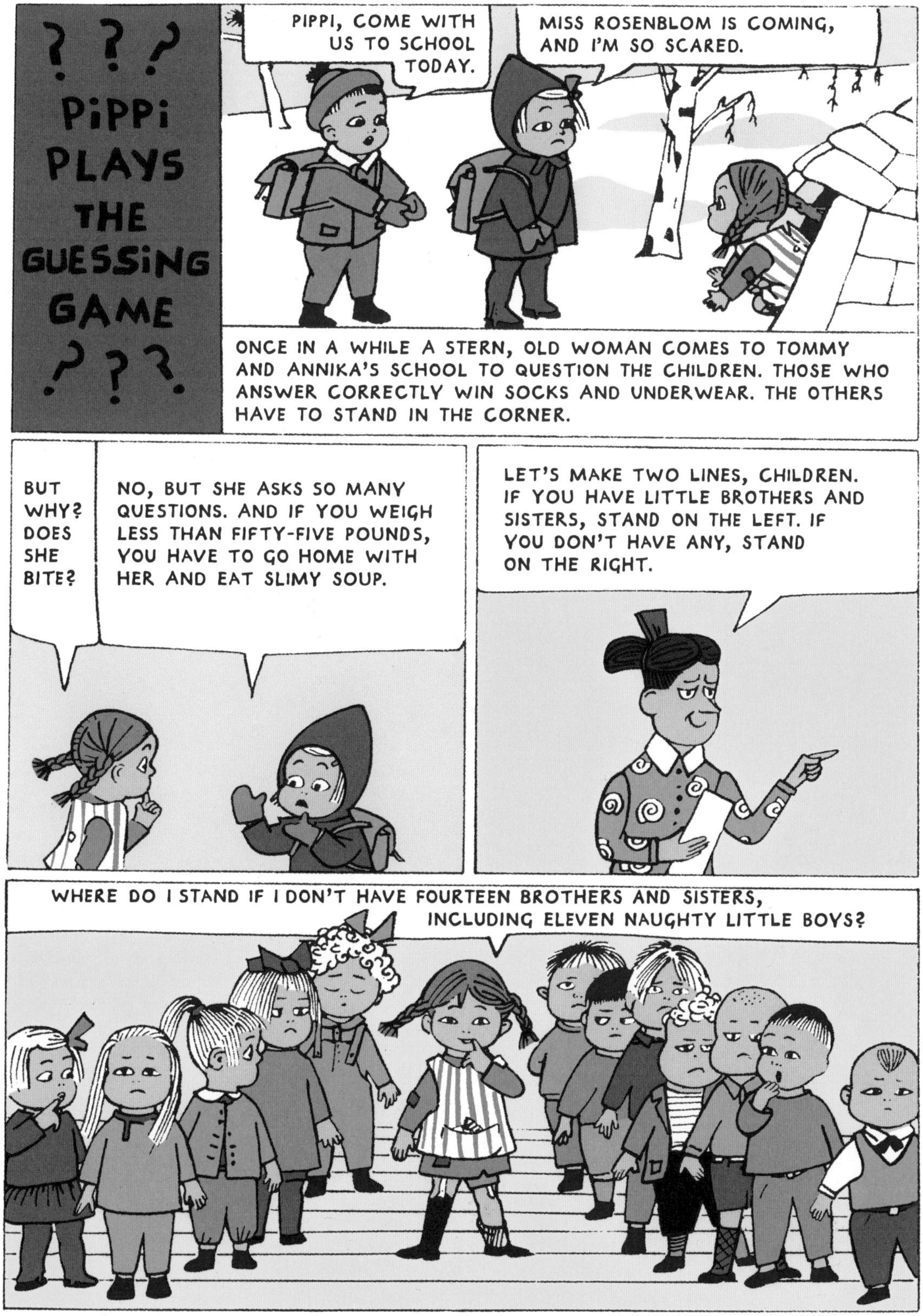
PIPPI PLAYS THE GUESSING GAME
PIPPI, COME WITH US TO SCHOOL TODAY.
MISS ROSENBLOM IS COMING, AND I'M SO SCARED.
ONCE IN A WHILE A STERN, OLD WOMAN COMES TO TOMMY AND ANNIKA'S SCHOOL TO QUESTION THE CHILDREN. THOSE WHO ANSWER CORRECTLY WIN SOCKS AND UNDERWEAR. THE OTHERS HAVE TO STAND IN THE CORNER.
BUT WHY? DOES SHE BITE?
NO, BUT SHE ASKS SO MANY QUESTIONS. AND IF YOU WEIGH LESS THAN FIFTY-FIVE POUNDS, YOU HAVE TO GO HOME WITH HER AND EAT SLIMY SOUP.
LET'S MAKE TWO LINES, CHILDREN. IF YOU HAVE LITTLE BROTHERS AND SISTERS, STAND ON THE LEFT. IF YOU DON'T HAVE ANY, STAND ON THE RIGHT.
WHERE DO I STAND IF I DON'T HAVE FOURTEEN BROTHERS AND SISTERS, INCLUDING ELEVEN NAUGHTY LITTLE BOYS?

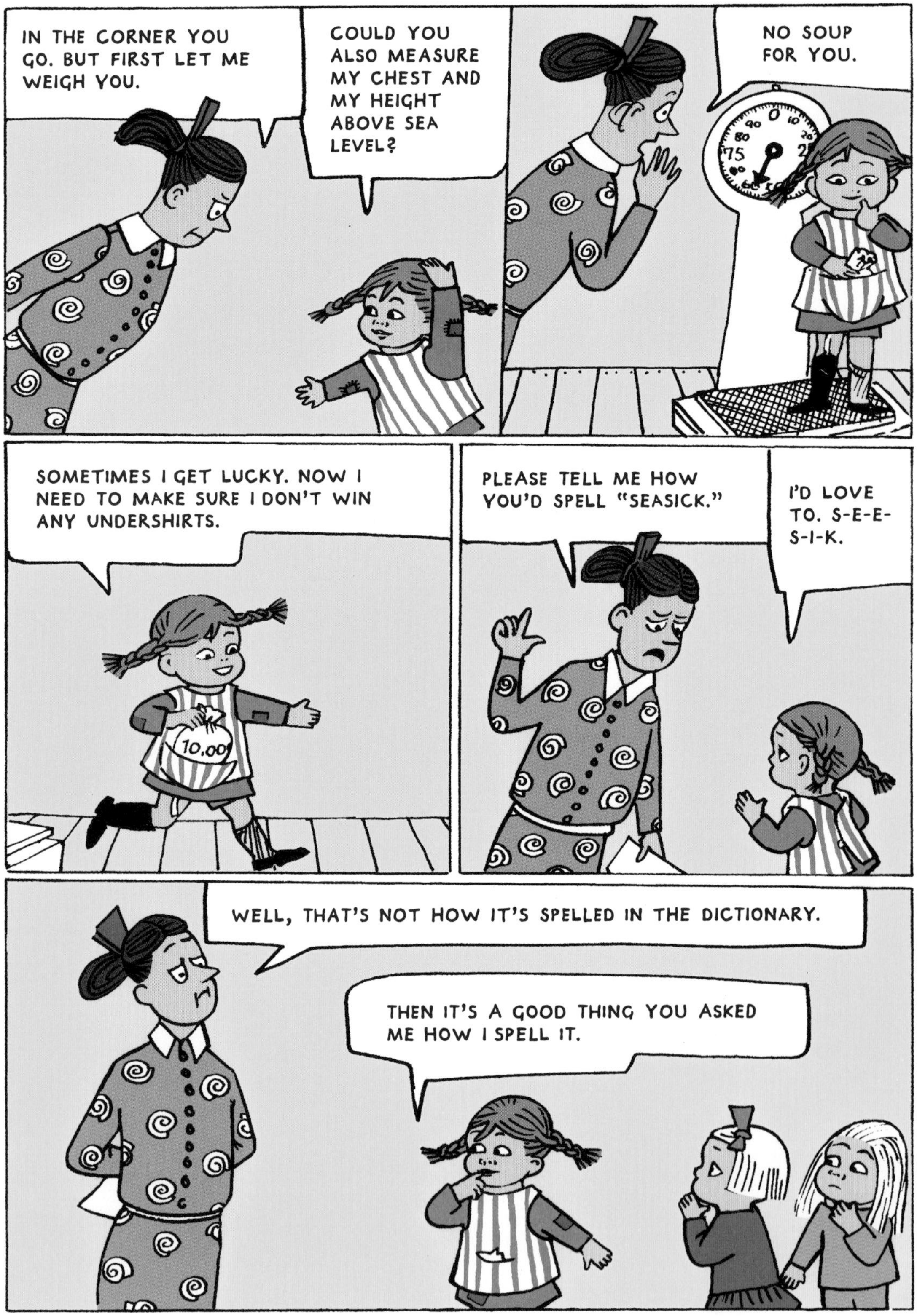
IN THE CORNER YOU GO. BUT FIRST LET ME WEIGH YOU.
COULD YOU ALSO MEASURE MY CHEST AND MY HEIGHT ABOVE SEA LEVEL?
NO SOUP FOR YOU.
SOMETIMES I GET LUCKY. NOW I NEED TO MAKE SURE I DON'T WIN ANY UNDERSHIRTS.
10,00
PLEASE TELL ME HOW YOU'D SPELL "SEASICK."
I'D LOVE TO. S-E-E-S-I-K.
WELL, THAT'S NOT HOW IT'S SPELLED IN THE DICTIONARY.
THEN IT'S A GOOD THING YOU ASKED ME HOW I SPELL IT.

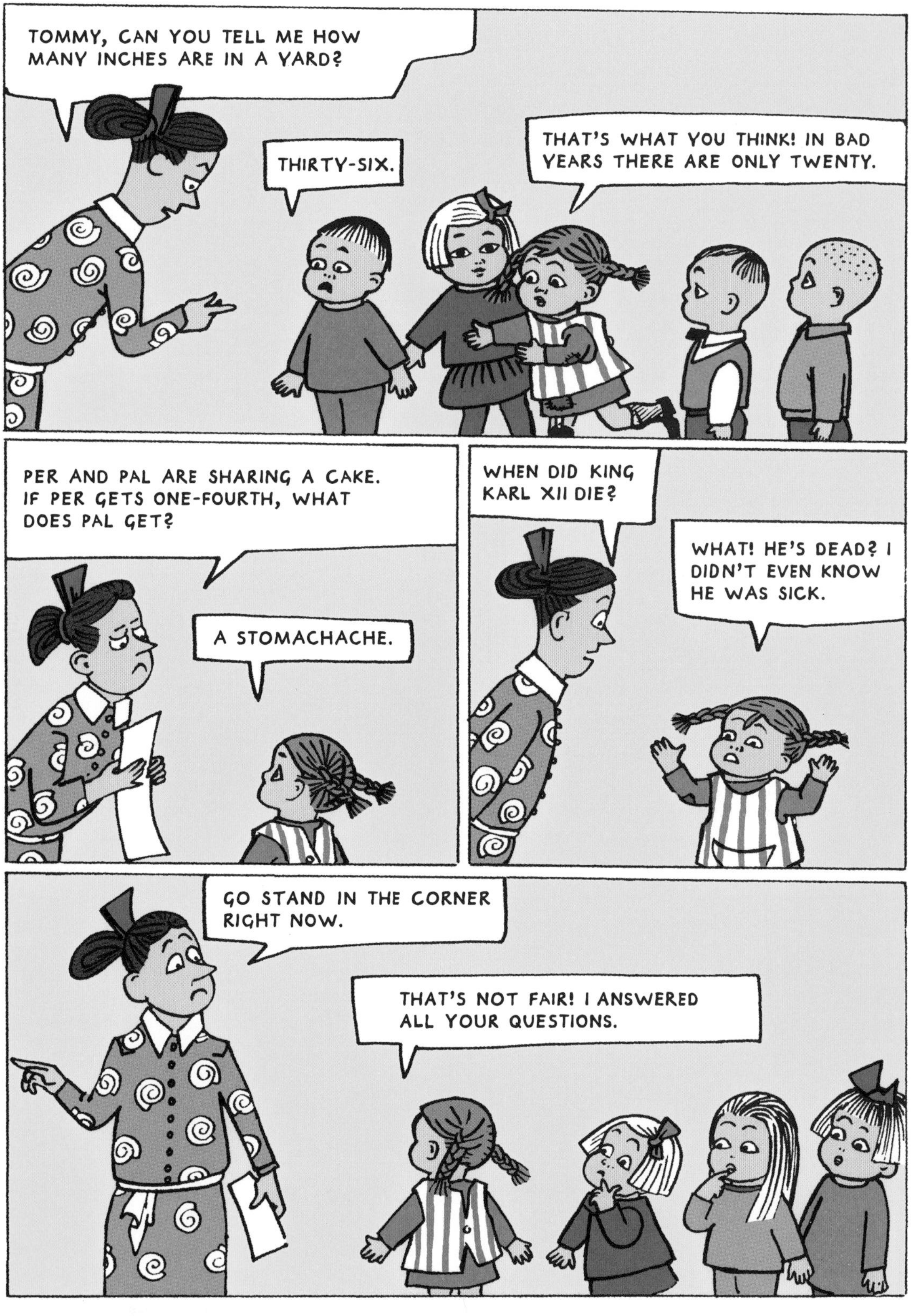
TOMMY, CAN YOU TELL ME HOW MANY INCHES ARE IN A YARD?
THIRTY-SIX.
THAT'S WHAT YOU THINK! IN BAD YEARS THERE ARE ONLY TWENTY.
PER AND PAL ARE SHARING A CAKE. IF PER GETS ONE-FOURTH, WHAT DOES PAL GET?
A STOMACHACHE.
WHEN DID KING KARL XII DIE?
WHAT! HE'S DEAD? I DIDN'T EVEN KNOW HE WAS SICK.
GO STAND IN THE CORNER RIGHT NOW.
THAT'S NOT FAIR! I ANSWERED ALL YOUR QUESTIONS.

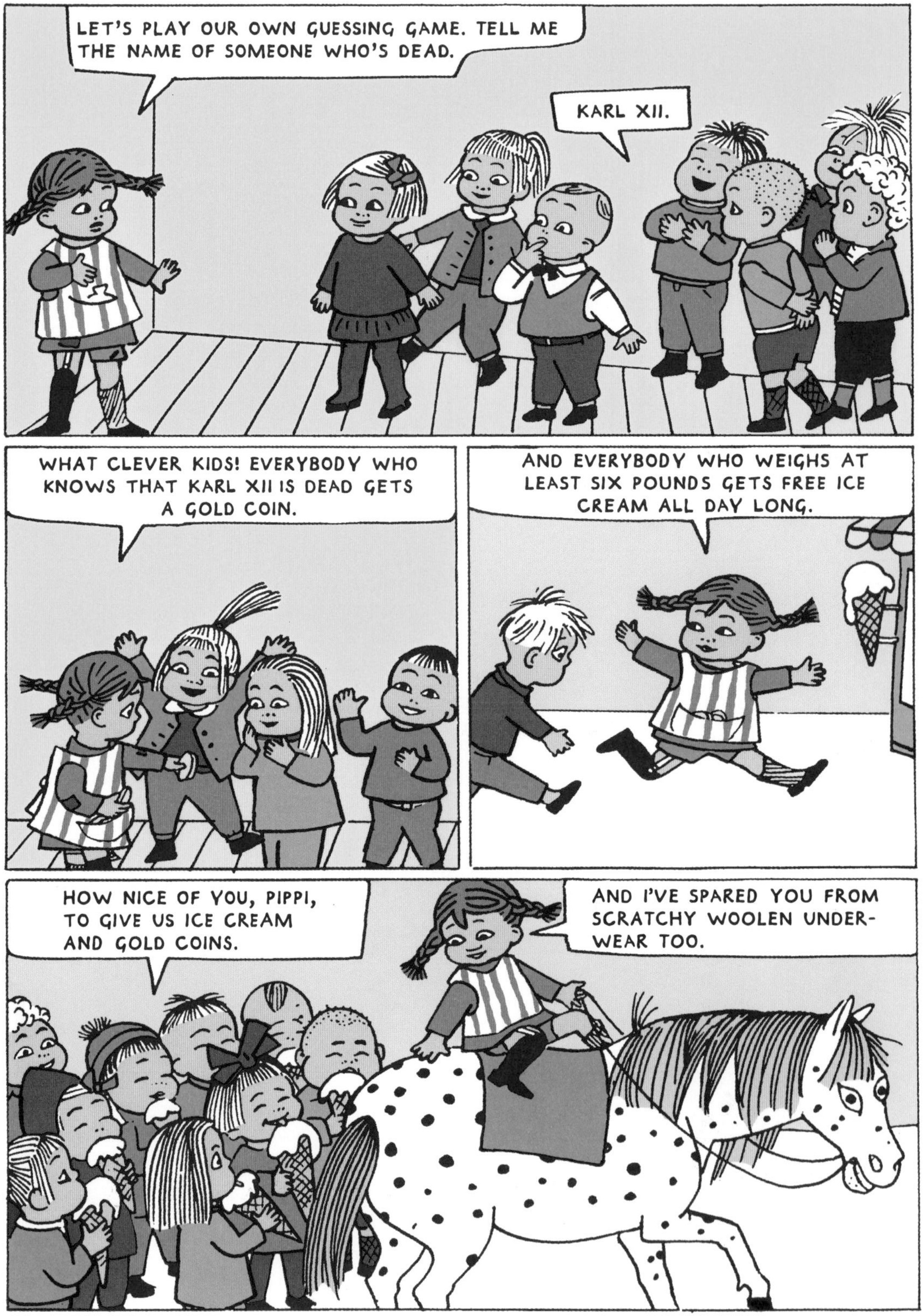
LET'S PLAY OUR OWN GUESSING GAME. TELL ME THE NAME OF SOMEONE WHO'S DEAD.
KARL XII.
WHAT CLEVER KIDS! EVERYBODY WHO KNOWS THAT KARL XII IS DEAD GETS A GOLD COIN.
AND EVERYBODY WHO WEIGHS AT LEAST SIX POUNDS GETS FREE ICE CREAM ALL DAY LONG.
HOW NICE OF YOU, PIPPI, TO GIVE US ICE CREAM AND GOLD COINS.
AND I'VE SPARED YOU FROM SCRATCHY WOOLEN UNDER-WEAR TOO.

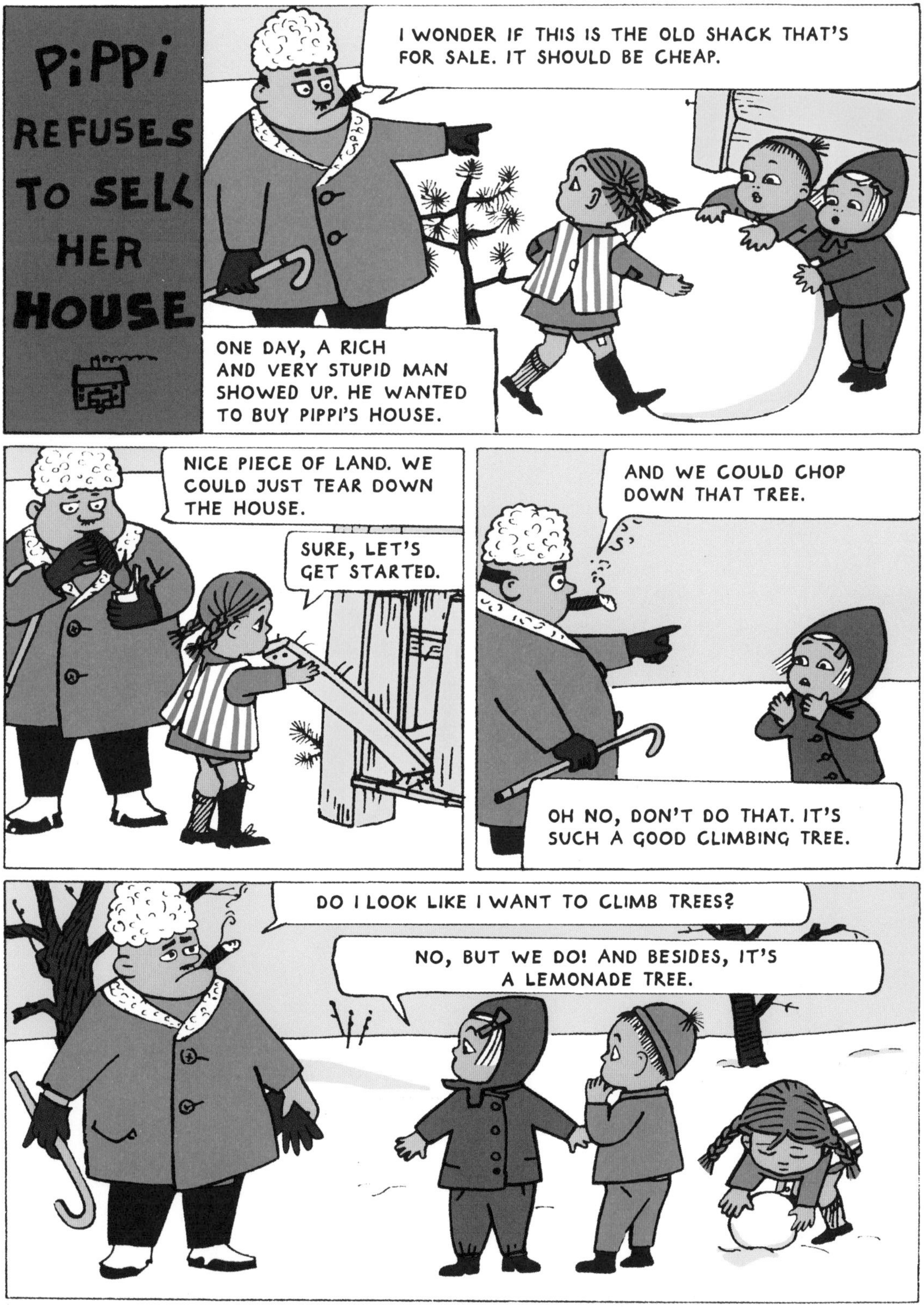
PIPPI REFUSES TO SELL HER HOUSE
I WONDER IF THIS IS THE OLD SHACK THAT'S FOR SALE. IT SHOULD BE CHEAP.
ONE DAY, A RICH AND VERY STUPID MAN SHOWED UP. HE WANTED TO BUY PIPPI'S HOUSE.
NICE PIECE OF LAND. WE COULD JUST TEAR DOWN THE HOUSE.
SURE, LET'S GET STARTED.
AND WE COULD CHOP DOWN THAT TREE.
OH NO, DON'T DO THAT. IT'S SUCH A GOOD CLIMBING TREE.
DO I LOOK LIKE I WANT TO CLIMB TREES?
NO, BUT WE DO! AND BESIDES, IT'S A LEMONADE TREE.

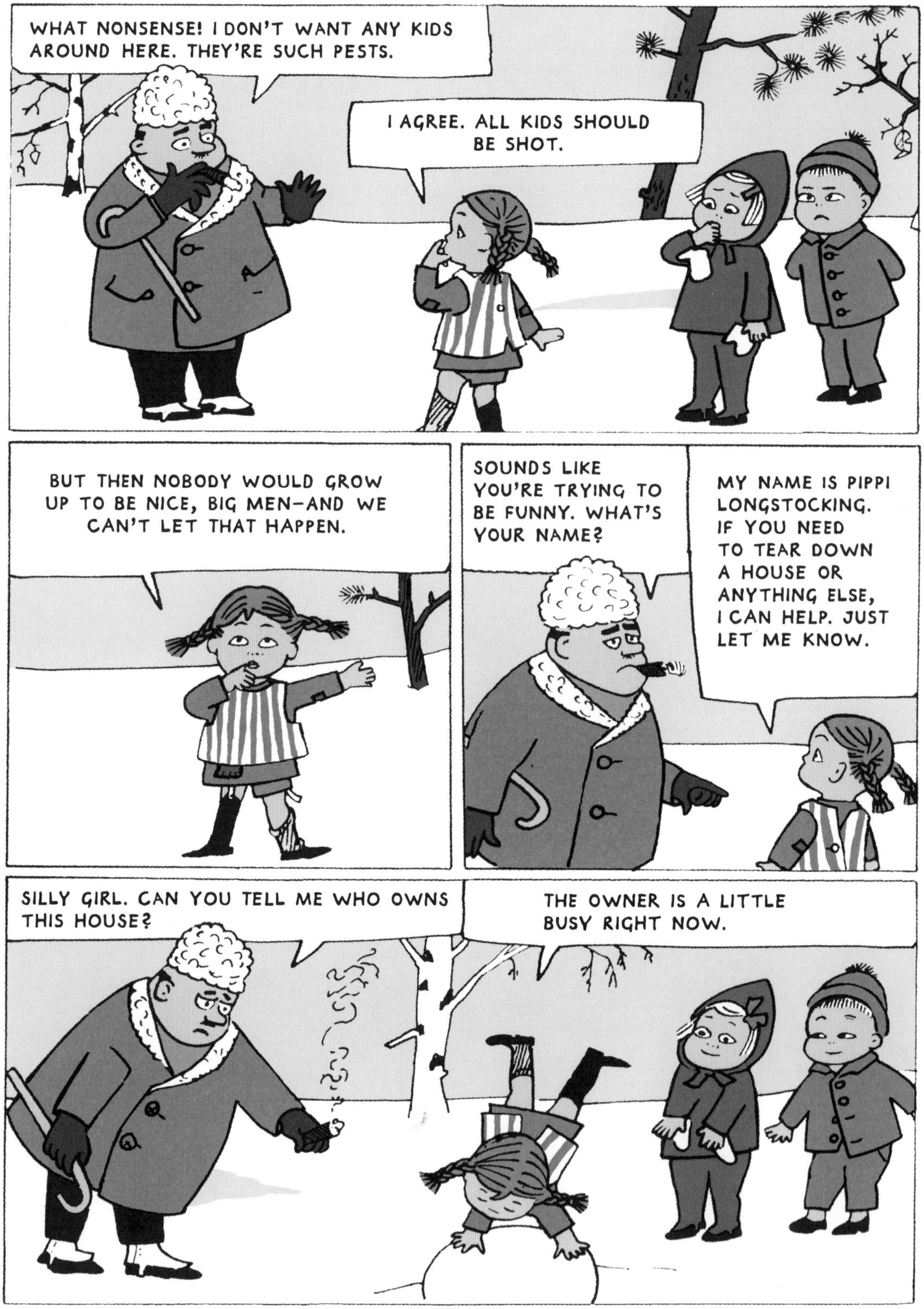
WHAT NONSENSE! I DON'T WANT ANY KIDS AROUND HERE. THEY'RE SUCH PESTS.
I AGREE. ALL KIDS SHOULD BE SHOT.
BUT THEN NOBODY WOULD GROW UP TO BE NICE, BIG MEN—AND WE CAN'T LET THAT HAPPEN.
SOUNDS LIKE YOU'RE TRYING TO BE FUNNY. WHAT'S YOUR NAME?
MY NAME IS PIPPI LONGSTOCKING. IF YOU NEED TO TEAR DOWN A HOUSE OR ANYTHING ELSE, I CAN HELP. JUST LET ME KNOW.
SILLY GIRL. CAN YOU TELL ME WHO OWNS THIS HOUSE?
THE OWNER IS A LITTLE BUSY RIGHT NOW.

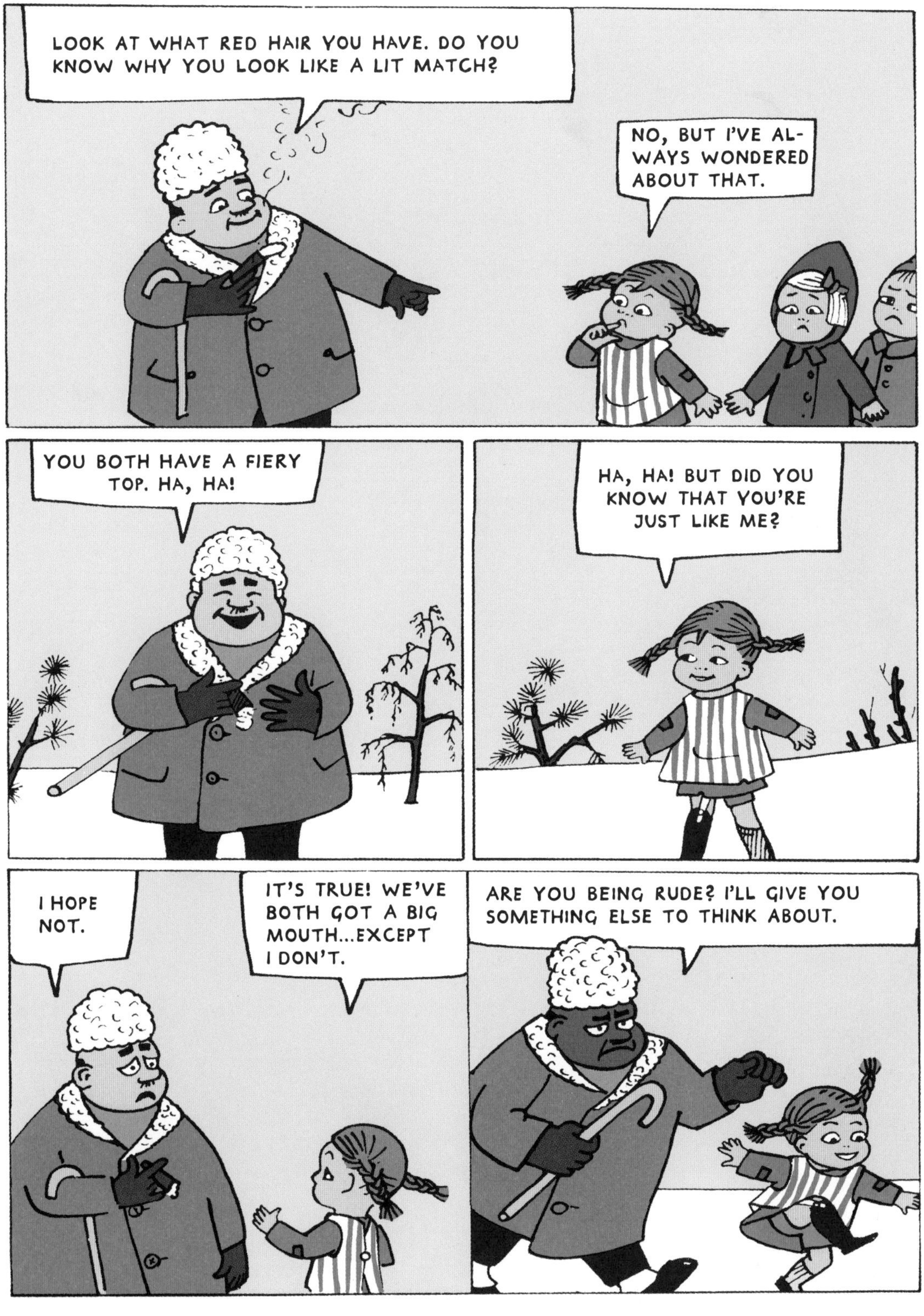
LOOK AT WHAT RED HAIR YOU HAVE. DO YOU KNOW WHY YOU LOOK LIKE A LIT MATCH?
NO, BUT I'VE ALWAYS WONDERED ABOUT THAT.
YOU BOTH HAVE A FIERY TOP. HA, HA!
HA, HA! BUT DID YOU KNOW THAT YOU'RE JUST LIKE ME?
I HOPE NOT.
IT'S TRUE! WE'VE BOTH GOT A BIG MOUTH...EXCEPT I DON'T.
ARE YOU BEING RUDE? I'LL GIVE YOU SOMETHING ELSE TO THINK ABOUT.

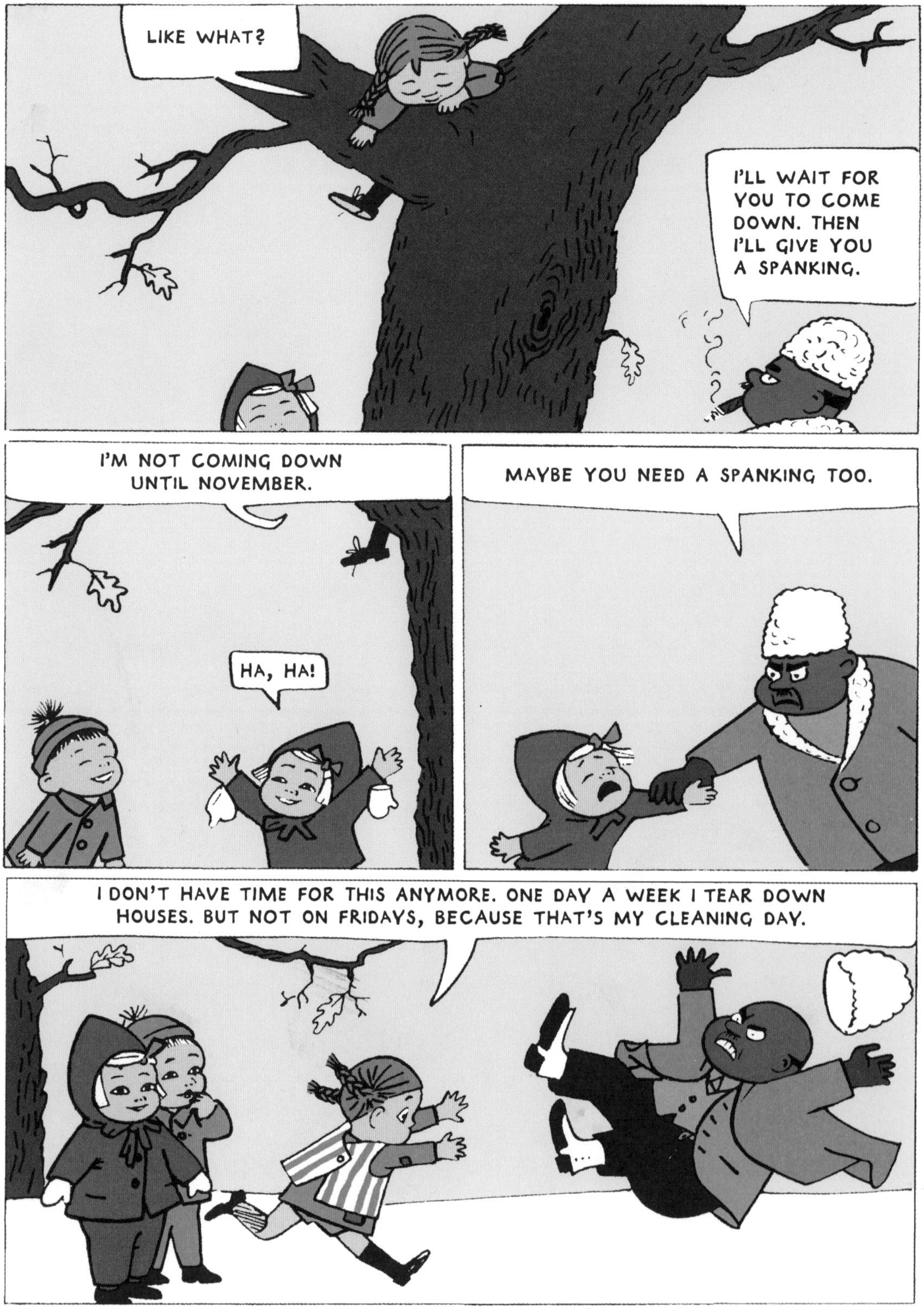
LIKE WHAT?
I'LL WAIT FOR YOU TO COME DOWN. THEN I'LL GIVE YOU A SPANKING.
I'M NOT COMING DOWN UNTIL NOVEMBER.
HA, HA!
MAYBE YOU NEED A SPANKING TOO.
I DON'T HAVE TIME FOR THIS ANYMORE. ONE DAY A WEEK I TEAR DOWN HOUSES. BUT NOT ON FRIDAYS, BECAUSE THAT'S MY CLEANING DAY.

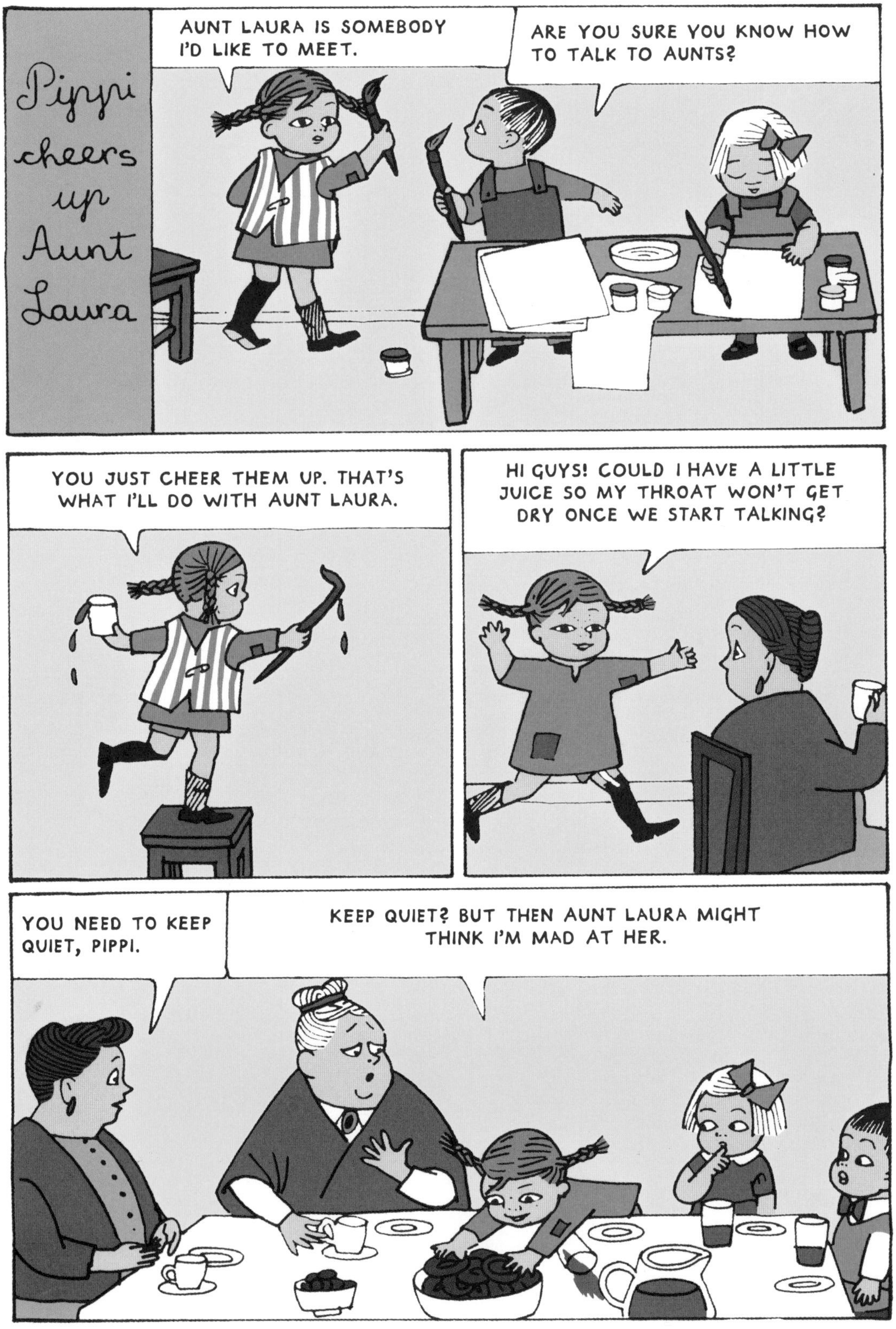
Pippi cheers up Aunt Laura
AUNT LAURA IS SOMEBODY I'D LIKE TO MEET.
ARE YOU SURE YOU KNOW HOW TO TALK TO AUNTS?
YOU JUST CHEER THEM UP. THAT'S WHAT I'LL DO WITH AUNT LAURA.
HI GUYS! COULD I HAVE A LITTLE JUICE SO MY THROAT WON'T GET DRY ONCE WE START TALKING?
YOU NEED TO KEEP QUIET, PIPPI.
KEEP QUIET? BUT THEN AUNT LAURA MIGHT THINK I'M MAD AT HER.

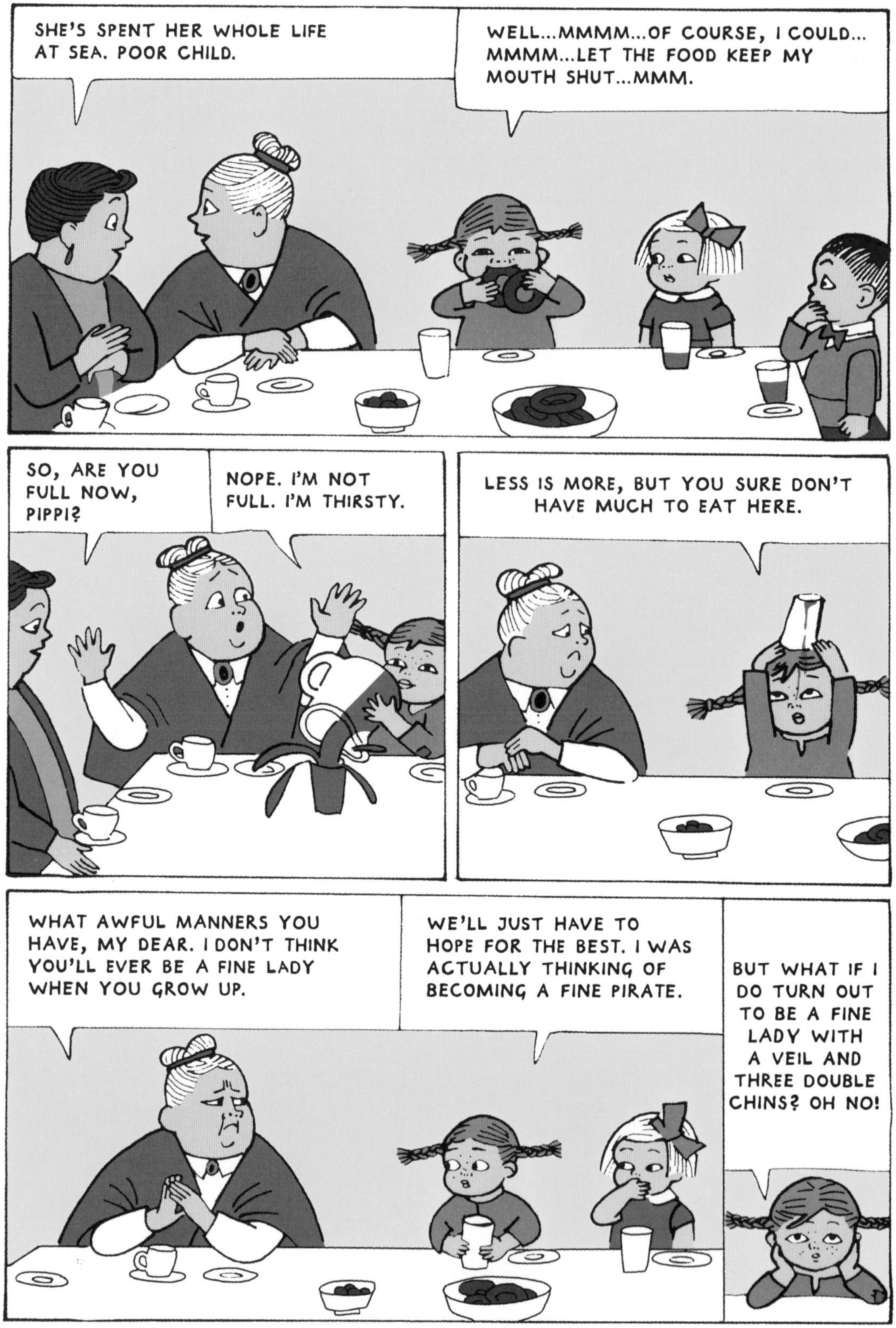
SHE'S SPENT HER WHOLE LIFE AT SEA. POOR CHILD.
WELL...MMMM...OF COURSE, I COULD... MMMM...LET THE FOOD KEEP MY MOUTH SHUT...MMM.
SO, ARE YOU FULL NOW, PIPPI?
NOPE. I'M NOT FULL. I'M THIRSTY.
LESS IS MORE, BUT YOU SURE DON'T HAVE MUCH TO EAT HERE.
WHAT AWFUL MANNERS YOU HAVE, MY DEAR. I DON'T THINK YOU'LL EVER BE A FINE LADY WHEN YOU GROW UP.
WE'LL JUST HAVE TO HOPE FOR THE BEST. I WAS ACTUALLY THINKING OF BECOMING A FINE PIRATE.
BUT WHAT IF I DO TURN OUT TO BE A FINE LADY WITH A VEIL AND THREE DOUBLE CHINS? OH NO!

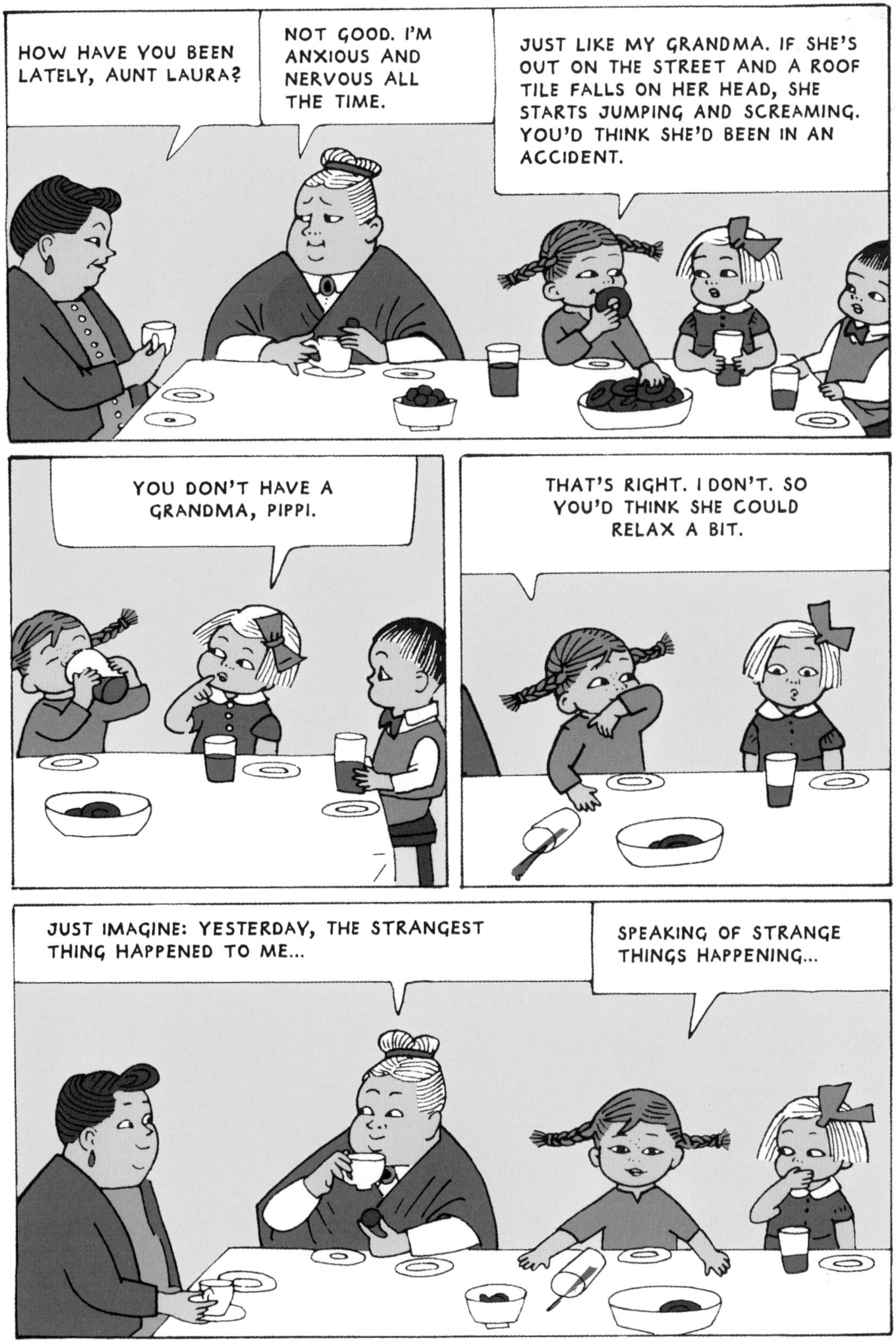
HOW HAVE YOU BEEN LATELY, AUNT LAURA?
NOT GOOD. I'M ANXIOUS AND NERVOUS ALL THE TIME.
JUST LIKE MY GRANDMA. IF SHE'S OUT ON THE STREET AND A ROOF TILE FALLS ON HER HEAD, SHE STARTS JUMPING AND SCREAMING. YOU'D THINK SHE'D BEEN IN AN ACCIDENT.
YOU DON'T HAVE A GRANDMA, PIPPI.
THAT'S RIGHT. I DON'T. SO YOU'D THINK SHE COULD RELAX A BIT.
JUST IMAGINE: YESTERDAY, THE STRANGEST THING HAPPENED TO ME...
SPEAKING OF STRANGE THINGS HAPPENING...

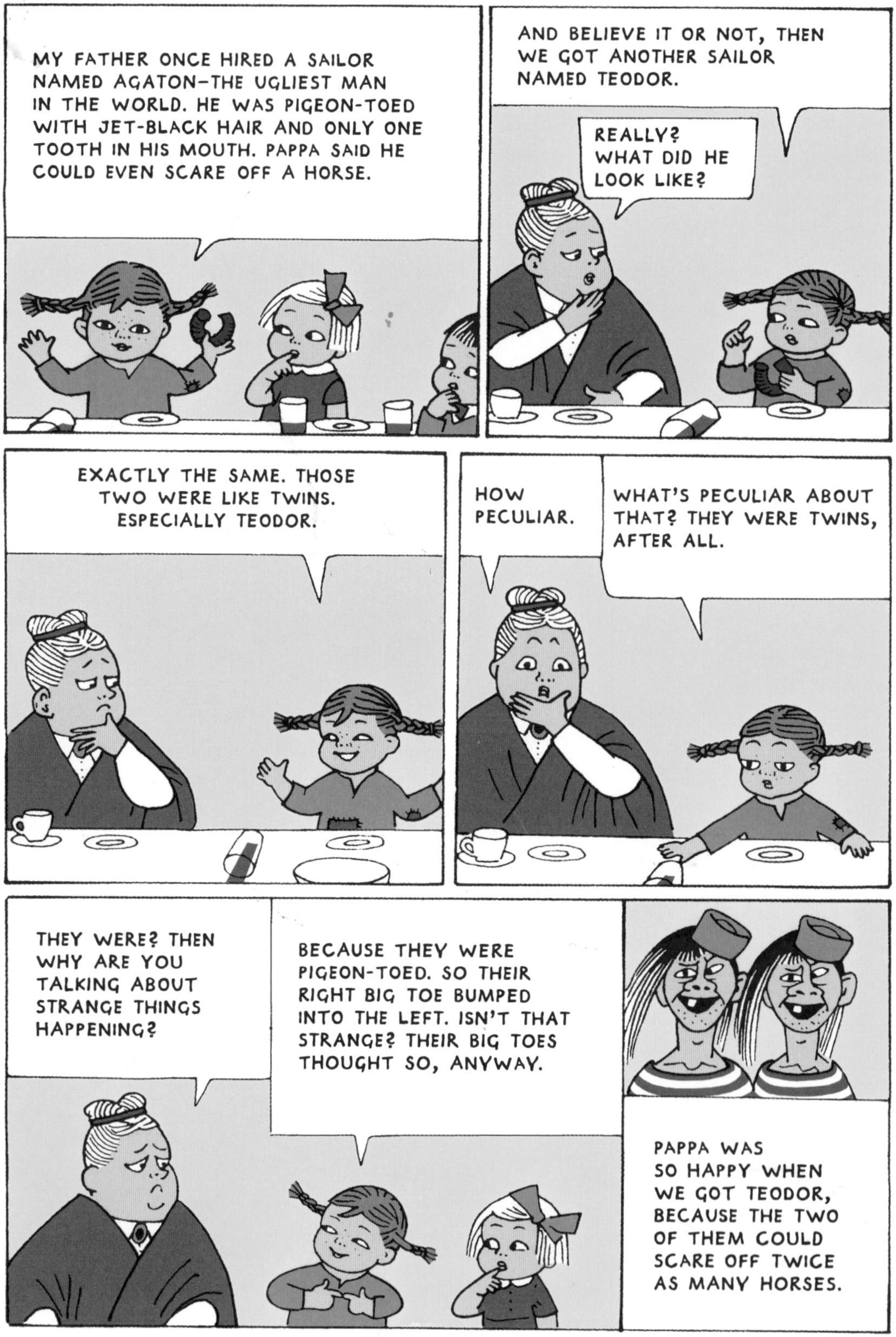
MY FATHER ONCE HIRED A SAILOR NAMED AGATON—THE UGLIEST MAN IN THE WORLD. HE WAS PIGEON-TOED WITH JET-BLACK HAIR AND ONLY ONE TOOTH IN HIS MOUTH. PAPPA SAID HE COULD EVEN SCARE OFF A HORSE.
AND BELIEVE IT OR NOT, THEN WE GOT ANOTHER SAILOR NAMED TEODOR.
REALLY? WHAT DID HE LOOK LIKE?
EXACTLY THE SAME. THOSE TWO WERE LIKE TWINS. ESPECIALLY TEODOR.
HOW PECULIAR.
WHAT'S PECULIAR ABOUT THAT? THEY WERE TWINS, AFTER ALL.
THEY WERE? THEN WHY ARE YOU TALKING ABOUT STRANGE THINGS HAPPENING?
BECAUSE THEY WERE PIGEON-TOED. SO THEIR RIGHT BIG TOE BUMPED INTO THE LEFT. ISN'T THAT STRANGE? THEIR BIG TOES THOUGHT SO, ANYWAY.
PAPPA WAS SO HAPPY WHEN WE GOT TEODOR, BECAUSE THE TWO OF THEM COULD SCARE OFF TWICE AS MANY HORSES.

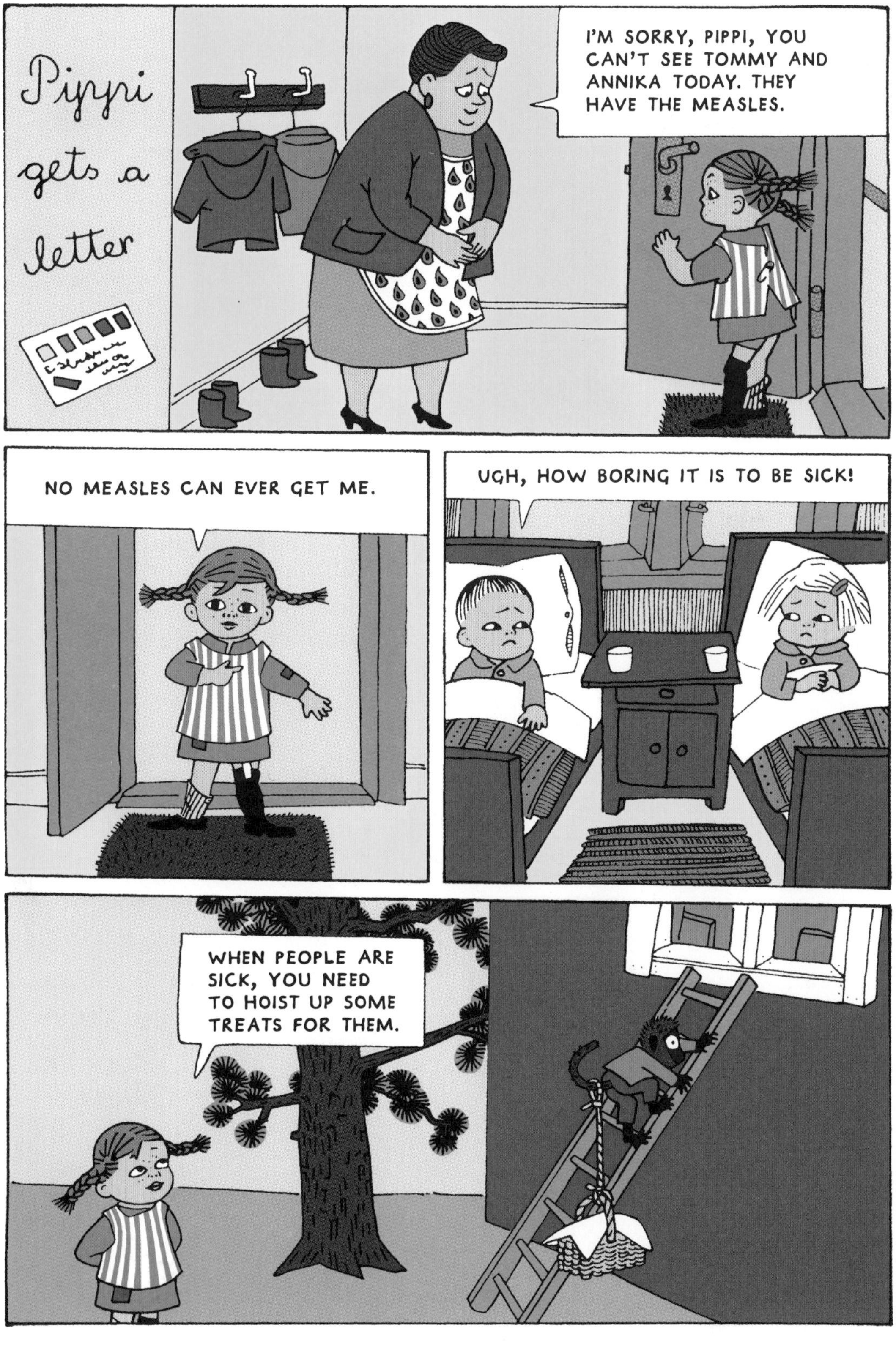
Pippi gets a letter
I'M SORRY, PIPPI, YOU CAN'T SEE TOMMY AND ANNIKA TODAY. THEY HAVE THE MEASLES.
NO MEASLES CAN EVER GET ME.
UGH, HOW BORING IT IS TO BE SICK!
WHEN PEOPLE ARE SICK, YOU NEED TO HOIST UP SOME TREATS FOR THEM.

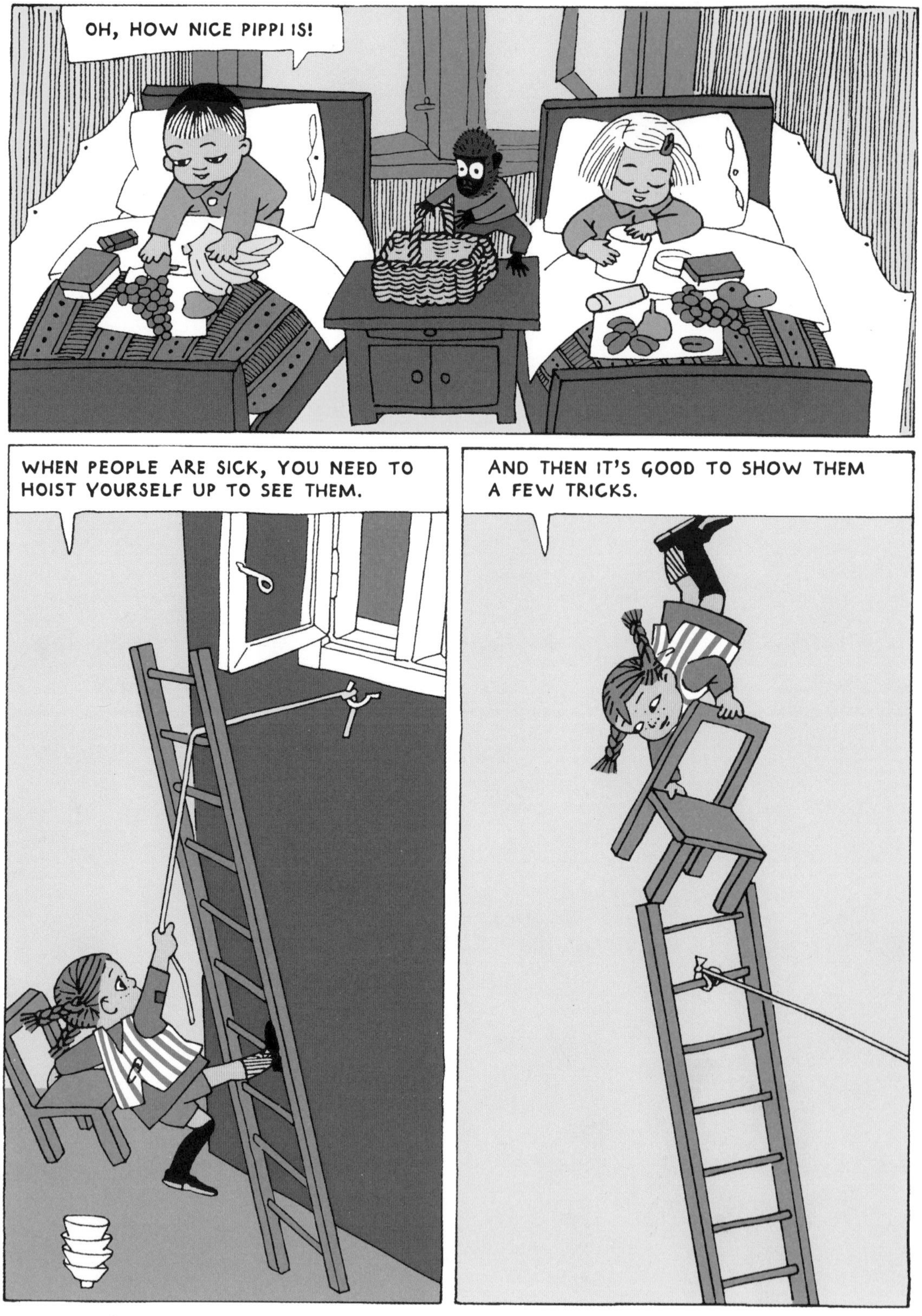
OH, HOW NICE PIPPI IS!
WHEN PEOPLE ARE SICK, YOU NEED TO HOIST YOURSELF UP TO SEE THEM.
AND THEN IT'S GOOD TO SHOW THEM A FEW TRICKS.

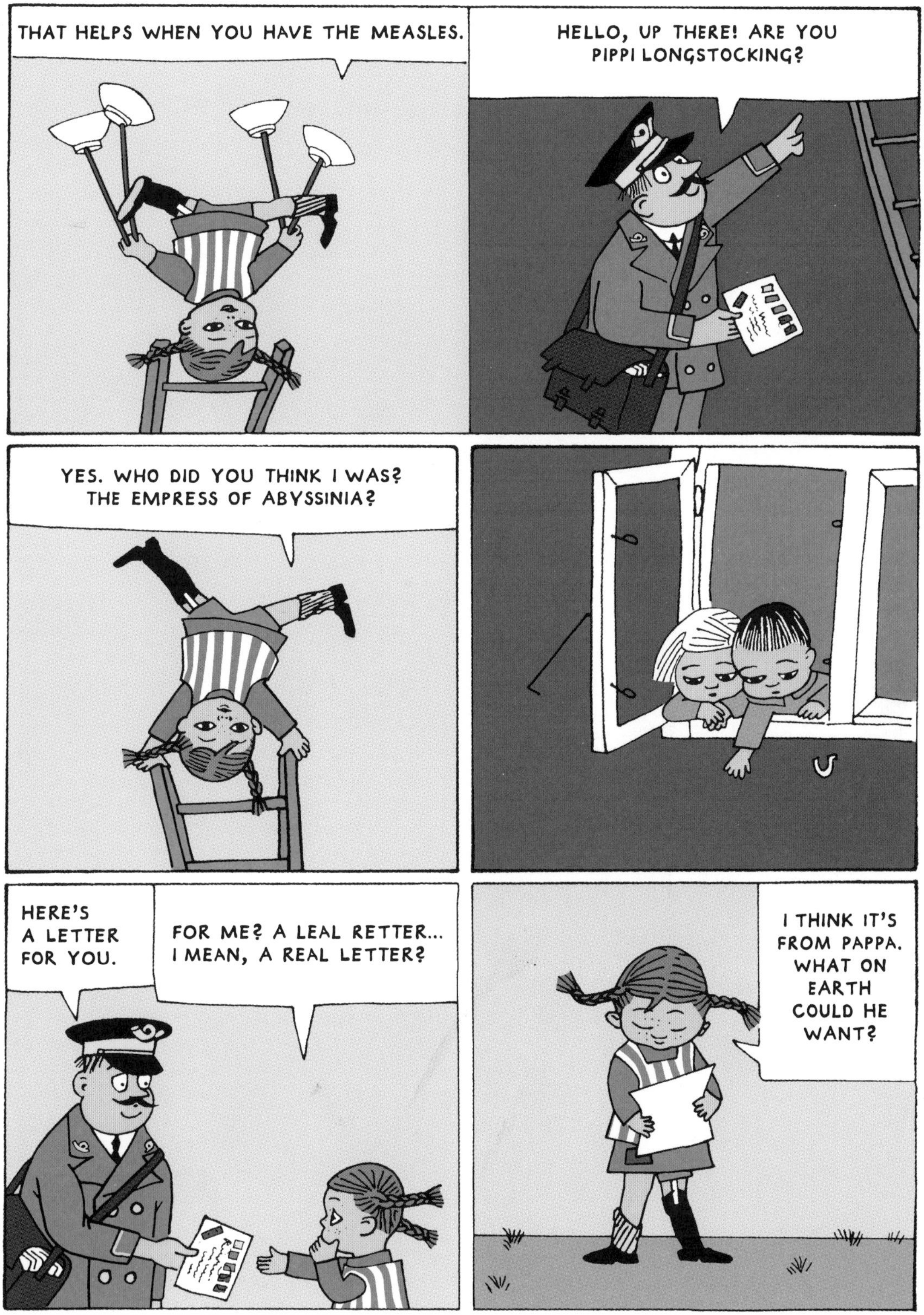

THAT HELPS WHEN YOU HAVE THE MEASLES.
HELLO, UP THERE! ARE YOU PIPPI LONGSTOCKING?
YES. WHO DID YOU THINK I WAS? THE EMPRESS OF ABYSSINIA?
HERE'S A LETTER FOR YOU.
FOR ME? A LEAL RETTER... I MEAN, A REAL LETTER?
I THINK IT'S FROM PAPPA. WHAT ON EARTH COULD HE WANT?

Dear Pippi,
Since your father is a South Seas king, you need to visit him now and then. So I'm sending you my boat to bring you here. Everyone is looking forward to meeting princess Pippilotta, and your father is too.
King Ephraim I Longstocking, ruler of Kurrakurradoot Island.
WHAT'S THIS? IS IT STARTING TO RAIN?
NO, ANNIKA'S CRYING.
DON'T CRY, ANNIKA. I THINK IT'LL BE FUN IN THE SOUTH SEAS.
FOR YOU, SURE.
TOMORROW YOU SHOULD BE WELL ENOUGH TO GET OUT OF BED.
I'M NEVER GETTING OUT OF BED NOW THAT PIPPI IS GOING AWAY.
JUST IMAGINE: A SOUTH SEAS PRINCESS!

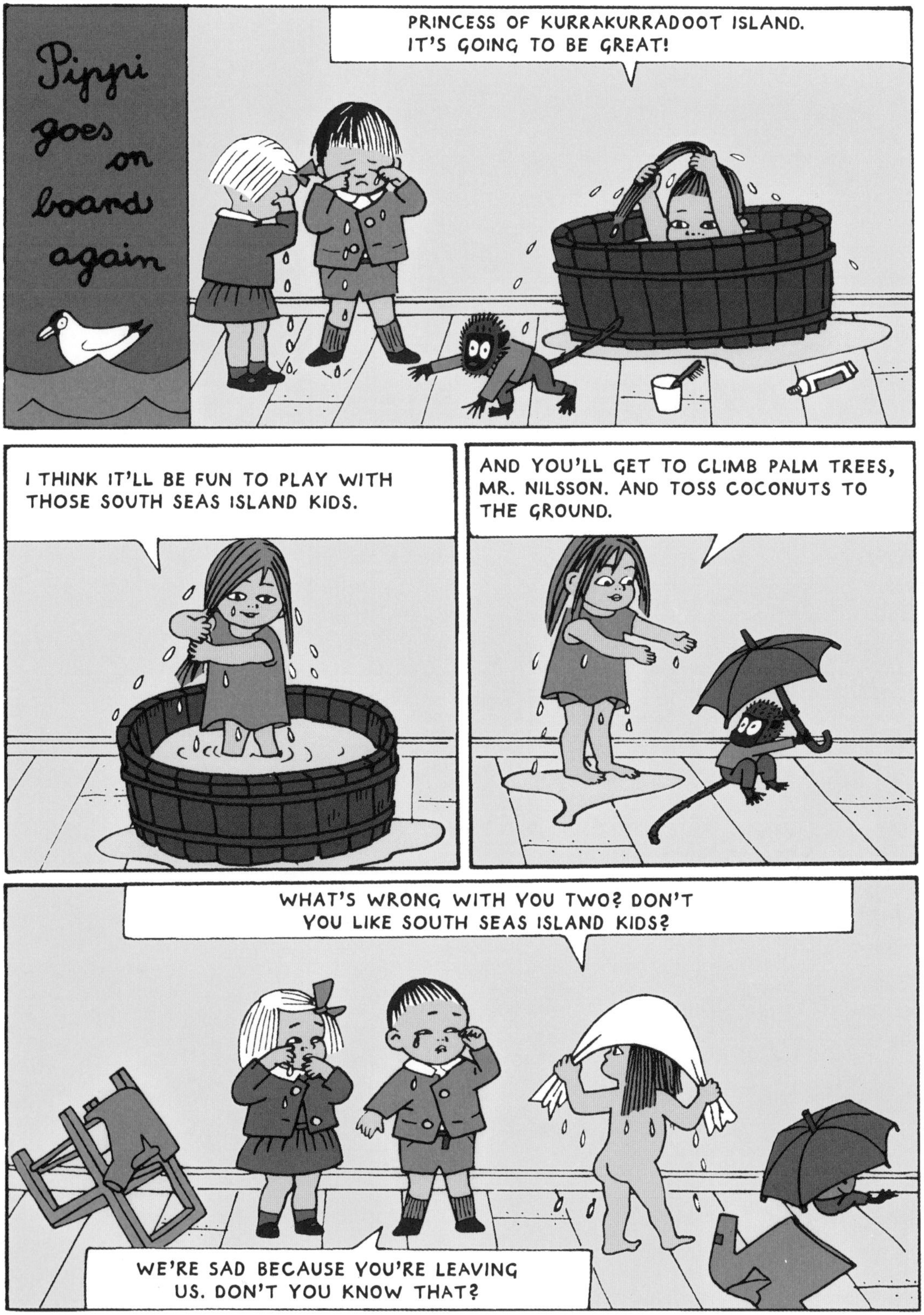
Pippi goes on board again
PRINCESS OF KURRAKURRADOOT ISLAND. IT'S GOING TO BE GREAT!
I THINK IT'LL BE FUN TO PLAY WITH THOSE SOUTH SEAS ISLAND KIDS.
AND YOU'LL GET TO CLIMB PALM TREES, MR. NILSSON. AND TOSS COCONUTS TO THE GROUND.
WHAT'S WRONG WITH YOU TWO? DON'T YOU LIKE SOUTH SEAS ISLAND KIDS?
WE'RE SAD BECAUSE YOU'RE LEAVING US. DON'T YOU KNOW THAT?

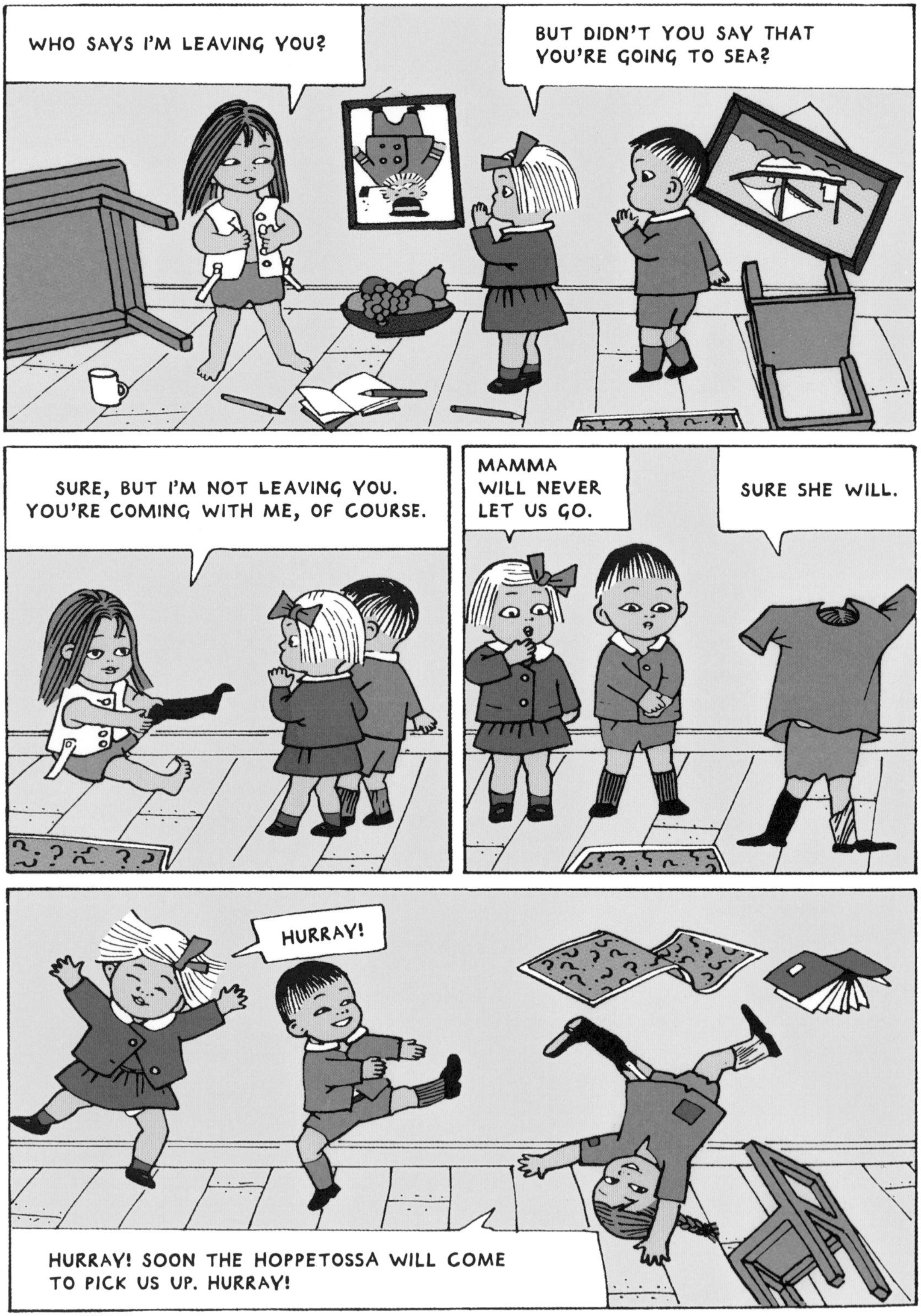
WHO SAYS I'M LEAVING YOU?
BUT DIDN'T YOU SAY THAT YOU'RE GOING TO SEA?
SURE, BUT I'M NOT LEAVING YOU. YOU'RE COMING WITH ME, OF COURSE.
MAMMA WILL NEVER LET US GO.
SURE SHE WILL.
HURRAY!
HURRAY! SOON THE HOPPETOSSA WILL COME TO PICK US UP. HURRAY!

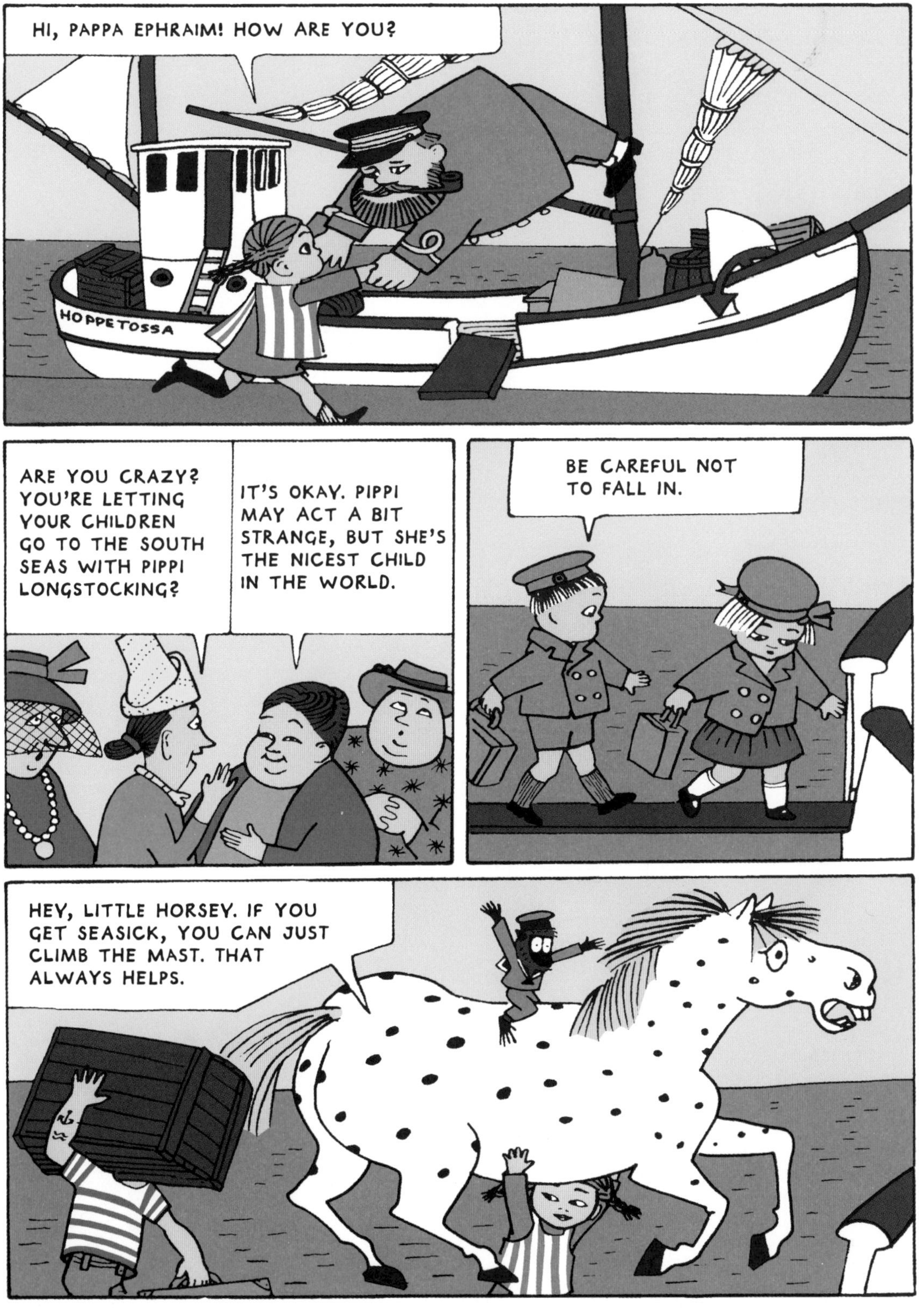
HI, PAPPA EPHRAIM! HOW ARE YOU?
HOPPETOSSA
ARE YOU CRAZY? YOU'RE LETTING YOUR CHILDREN GO TO THE SOUTH SEAS WITH PIPPI LONGSTOCKING?
IT'S OKAY. PIPPI MAY ACT A BIT STRANGE, BUT SHE'S THE NICEST CHILD IN THE WORLD.
BE CAREFUL NOT TO FALL IN.
HEY, LITTLE HORSEY. IF YOU GET SEASICK, YOU CAN JUST CLIMB THE MAST. THAT ALWAYS HELPS.

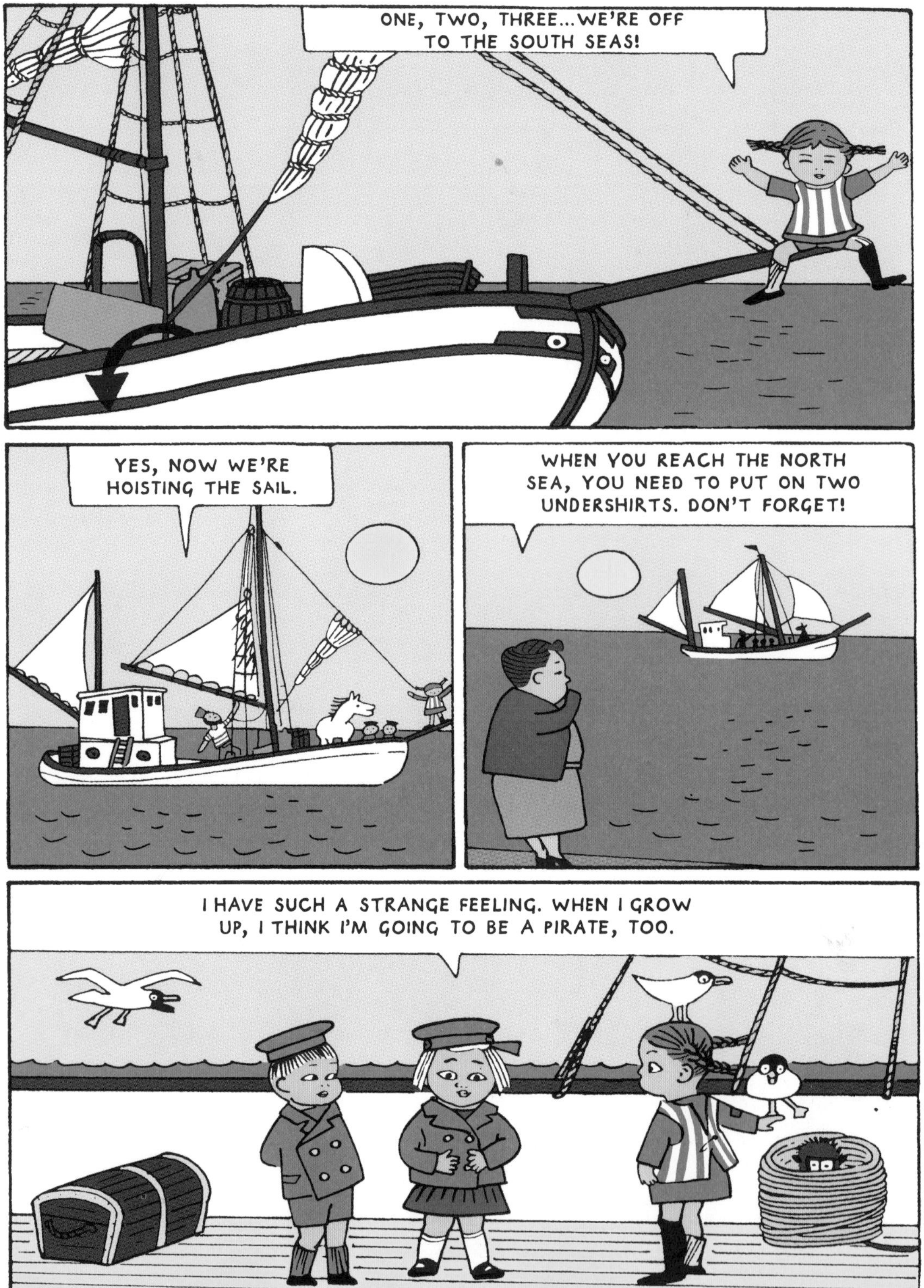
ONE, TWO, THREE...WE'RE OFF TO THE SOUTH SEAS!
YES, NOW WE'RE HOISTING THE SAIL.
WHEN YOU REACH THE NORTH SEA, YOU NEED TO PUT ON TWO UNDERSHIRTS. DON'T FORGET!
I HAVE SUCH A STRANGE FEELING. WHEN I GROW UP, I THINK I'M GOING TO BE A PIRATE, TOO.

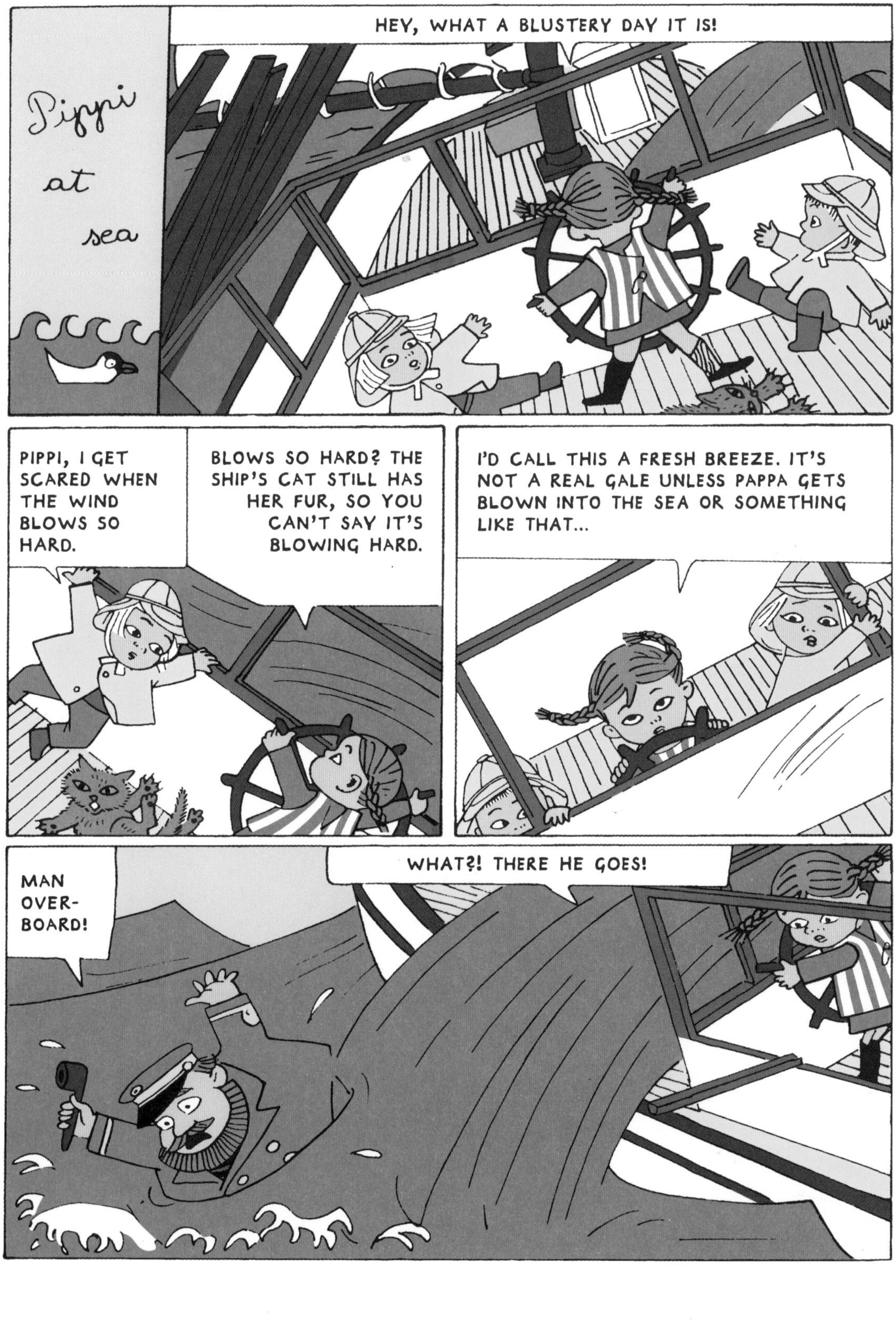
Pippi at sea
HEY, WHAT A BLUSTERY DAY IT IS!
PIPPI, I GET SCARED WHEN THE WIND BLOWS SO HARD.
BLOWS SO HARD? THE SHIP'S CAT STILL HAS HER FUR, SO YOU CAN'T SAY IT'S BLOWING HARD.
I'D CALL THIS A FRESH BREEZE. IT'S NOT A REAL GALE UNLESS PAPPA GETS BLOWN INTO THE SEA OR SOMETHING LIKE THAT...
MAN OVER-BOARD!
WHAT?! THERE HE GOES!

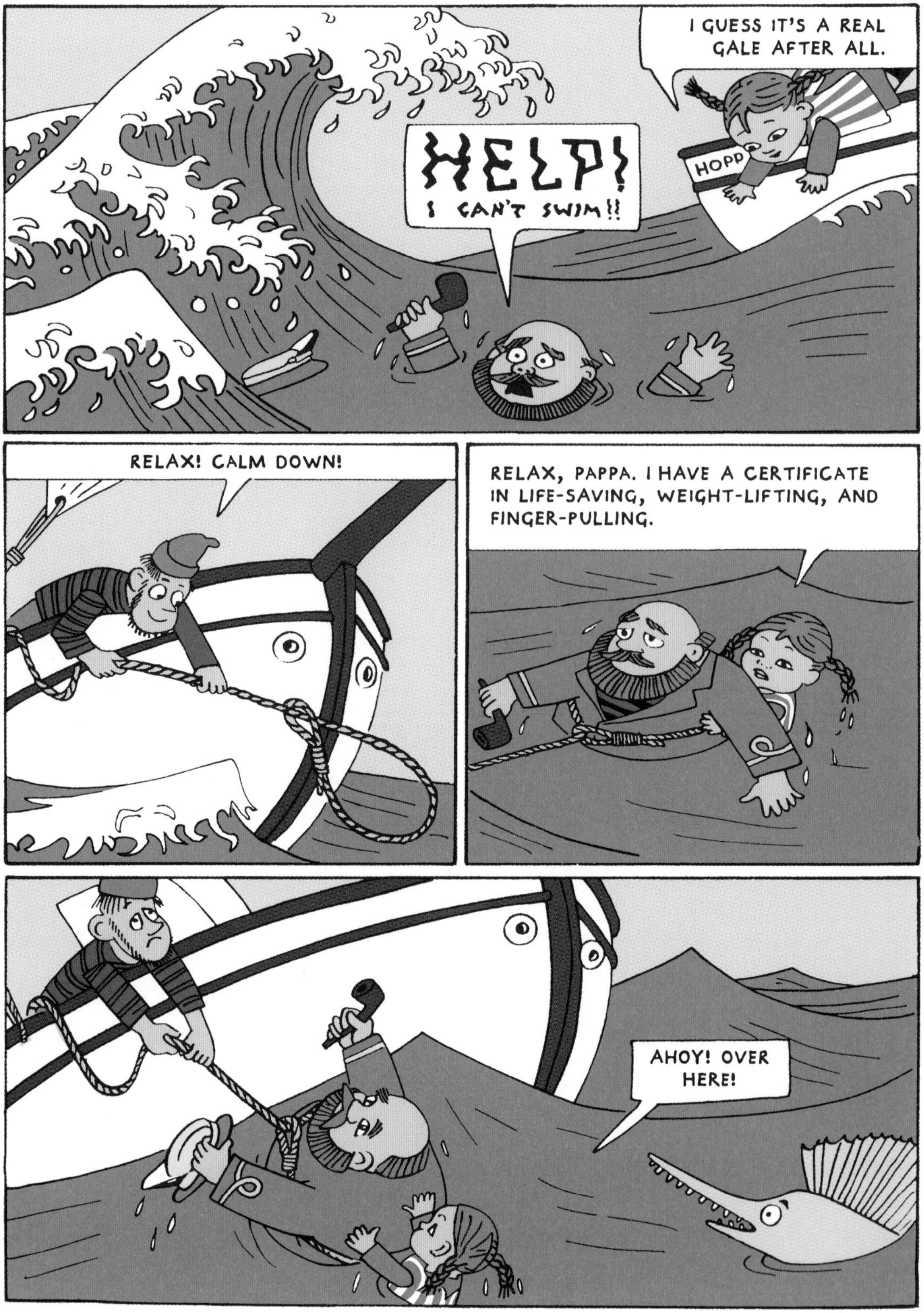
I GUESS IT'S A REAL GALE AFTER ALL.
HOPP
HELP! I CAN'T SWIM!!
RELAX! CALM DOWN!
RELAX, PAPPA. I HAVE A CERTIFICATE IN LIFE-SAVING, WEIGHT-LIFTING, AND FINGER-PULLING.
AHOY! OVER HERE!

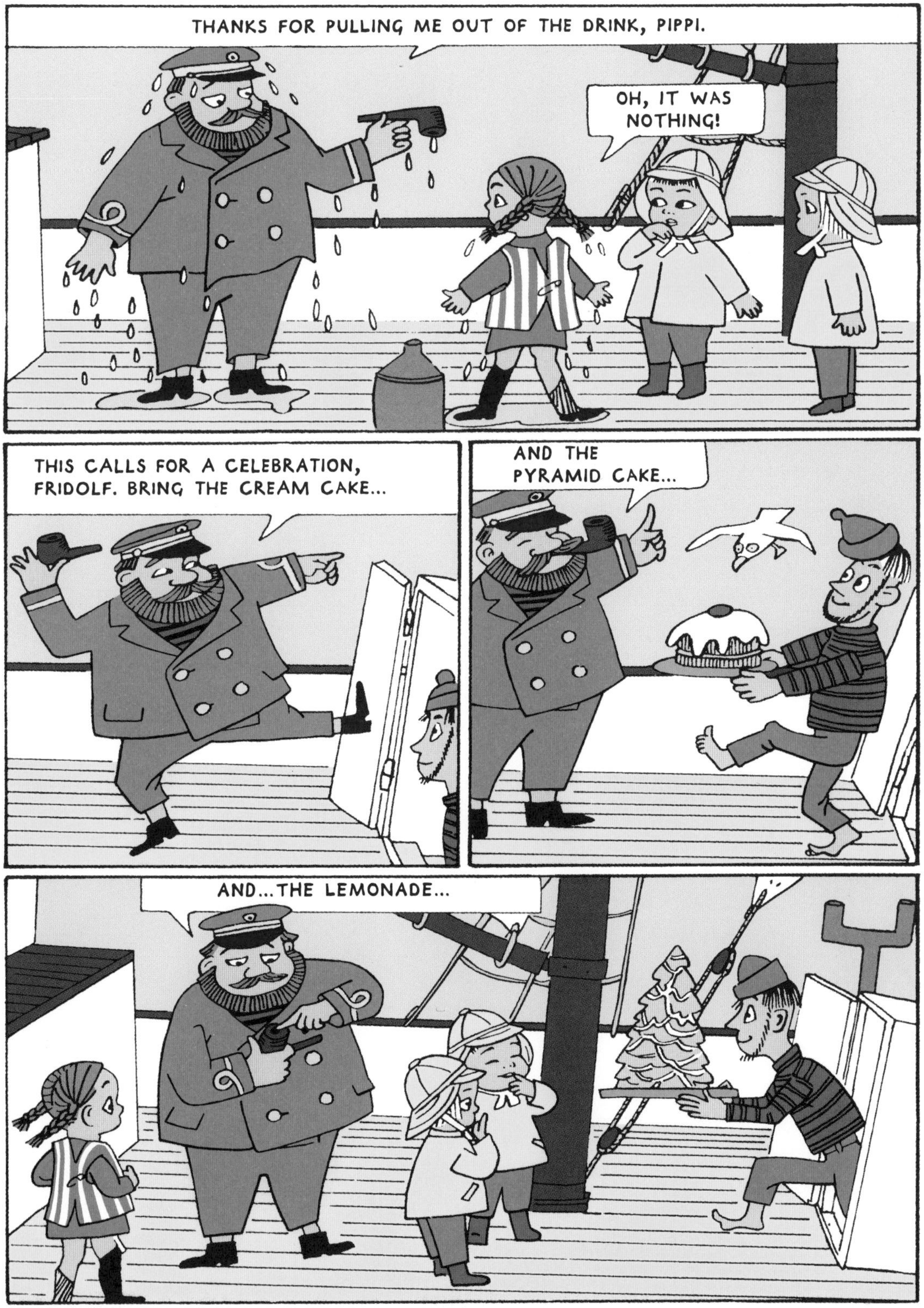
THANKS FOR PULLING ME OUT OF THE DRINK, PIPPI.
OH, IT WAS NOTHING!
THIS CALLS FOR A CELEBRATION, FRIDOLF. BRING THE CREAM CAKE...
AND THE PYRAMID CAKE...
AND...THE LEMONADE...

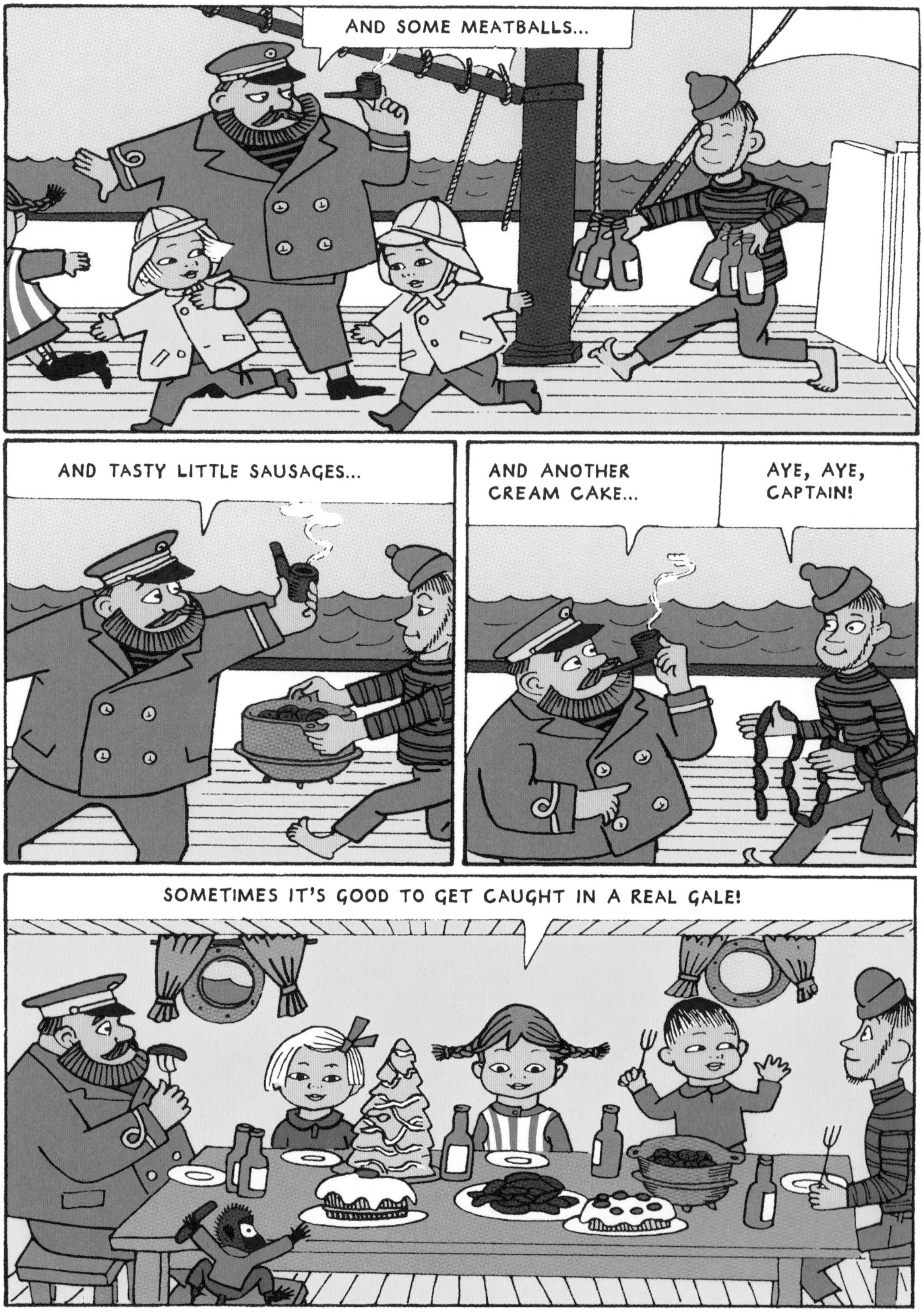
AND SOME MEATBALLS...
AND TASTY LITTLE SAUSAGES...
AND ANOTHER CREAM CAKE...
AYE, AYE, CAPTAIN!
SOMETIMES IT'S GOOD TO GET CAUGHT IN A REAL GALE!

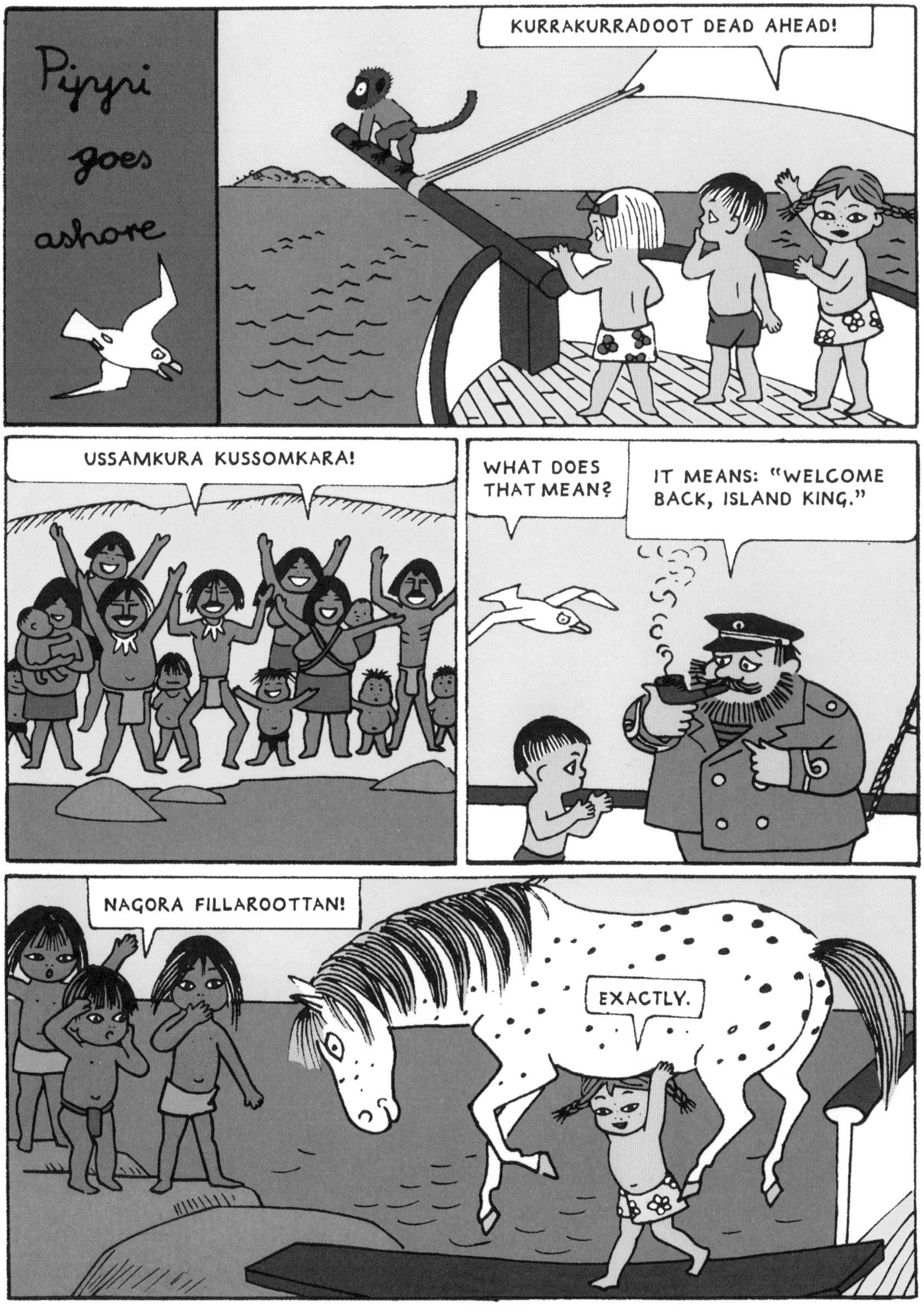
Pippi goes ashore
KURRAKURRADOOT DEAD AHEAD!
USSAMKURA KUSSOMKARA!
WHAT DOES THAT MEAN?
IT MEANS: "WELCOME BACK, ISLAND KING."
NAGORA FILLAROOTTAN!
EXACTLY.

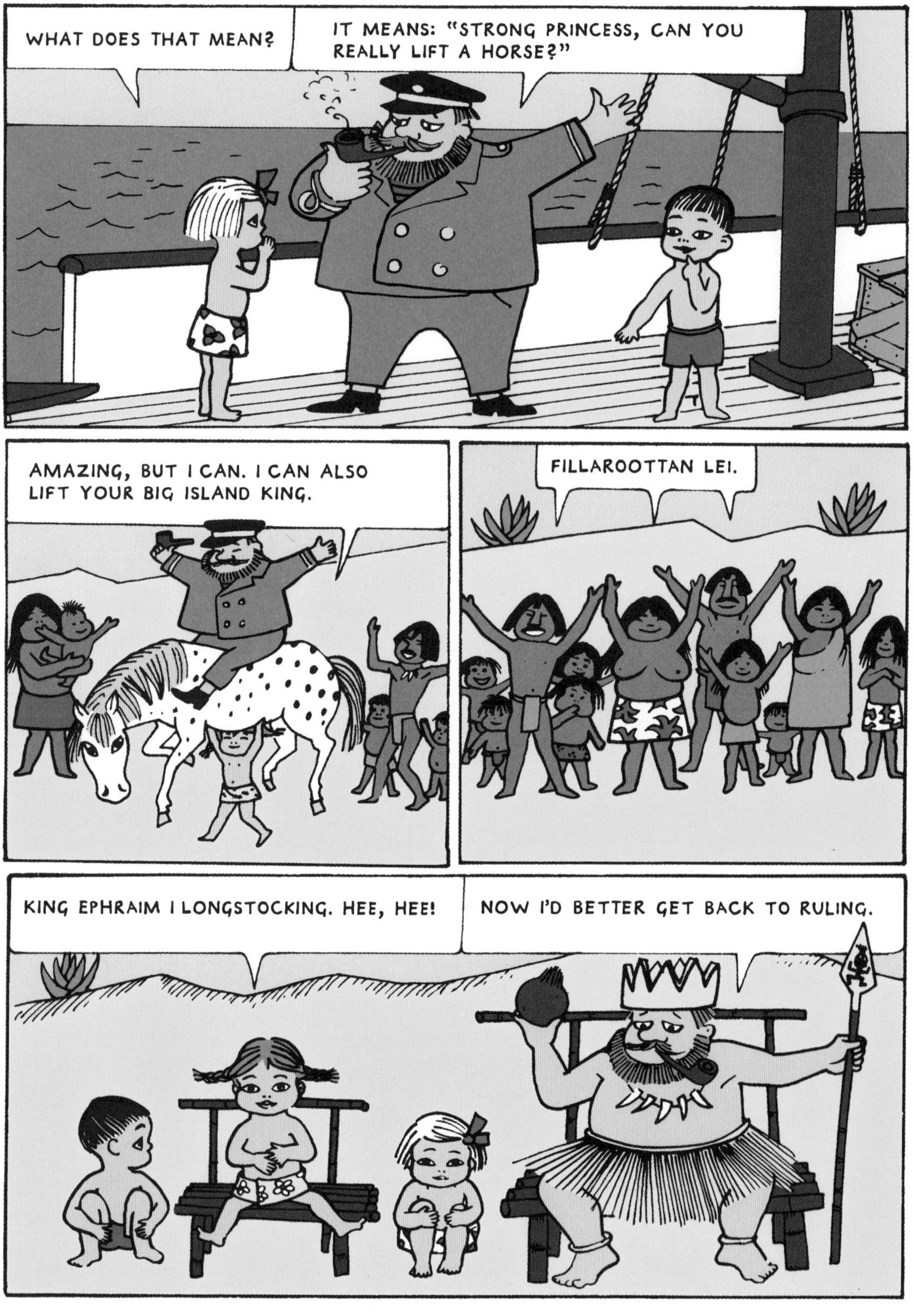
WHAT DOES THAT MEAN?
IT MEANS: "STRONG PRINCESS, CAN YOU REALLY LIFT A HORSE?"
AMAZING, BUT I CAN. I CAN ALSO LIFT YOUR BIG ISLAND KING.
FILLAROOTTAN LEI.
KING EPHRAIM I LONGSTOCKING. HEE, HEE!
NOW I'D BETTER GET BACK TO RULING.

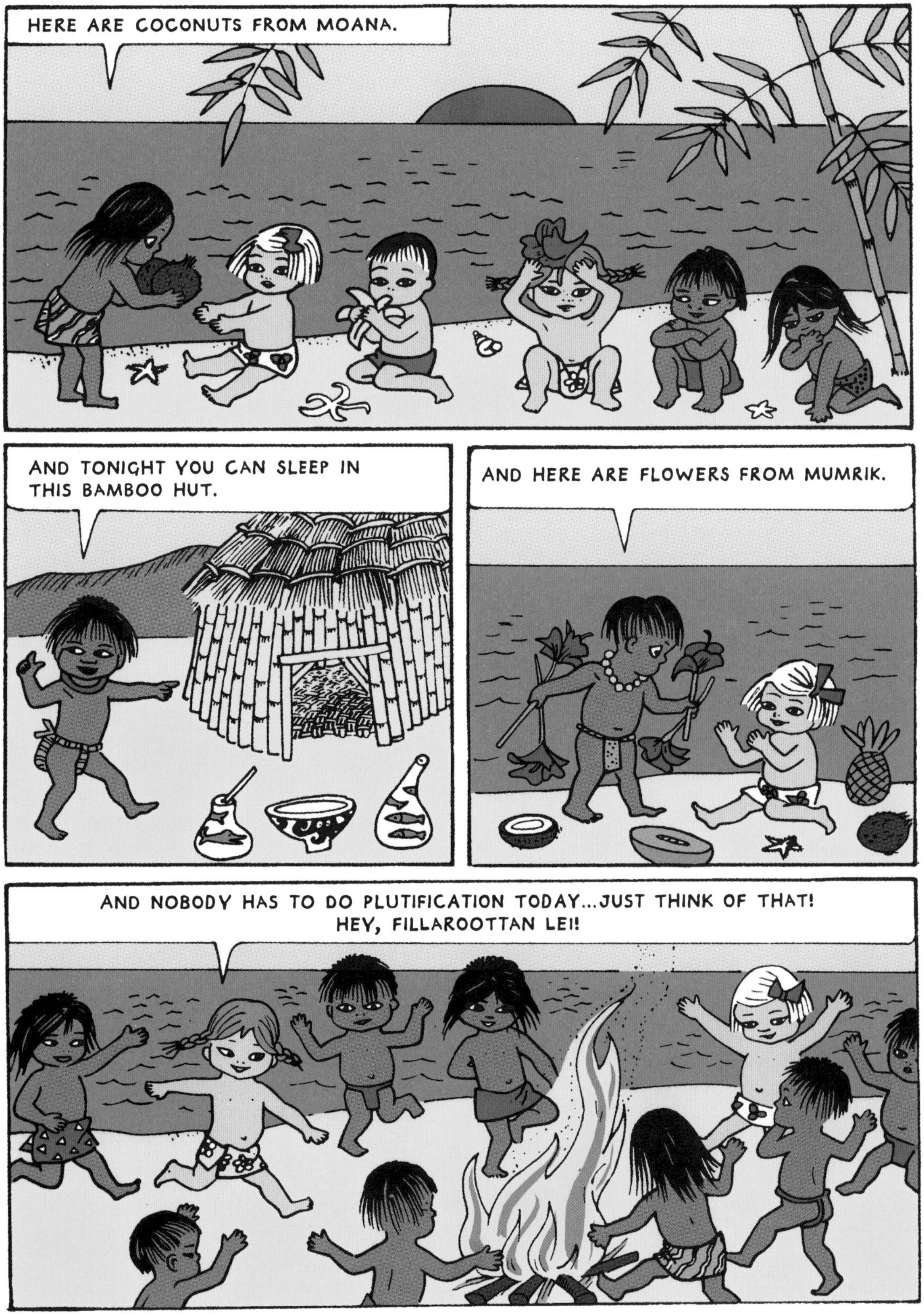
HERE ARE COCONUTS FROM MOANA.
AND TONIGHT YOU CAN SLEEP IN THIS BAMBOO HUT.
AND HERE ARE FLOWERS FROM MUMRIK.
AND NOBODY HAS TO DO PLUTIFICATION TODAY...JUST THINK OF THAT! HEY, FILLAROOTTAN LEI!

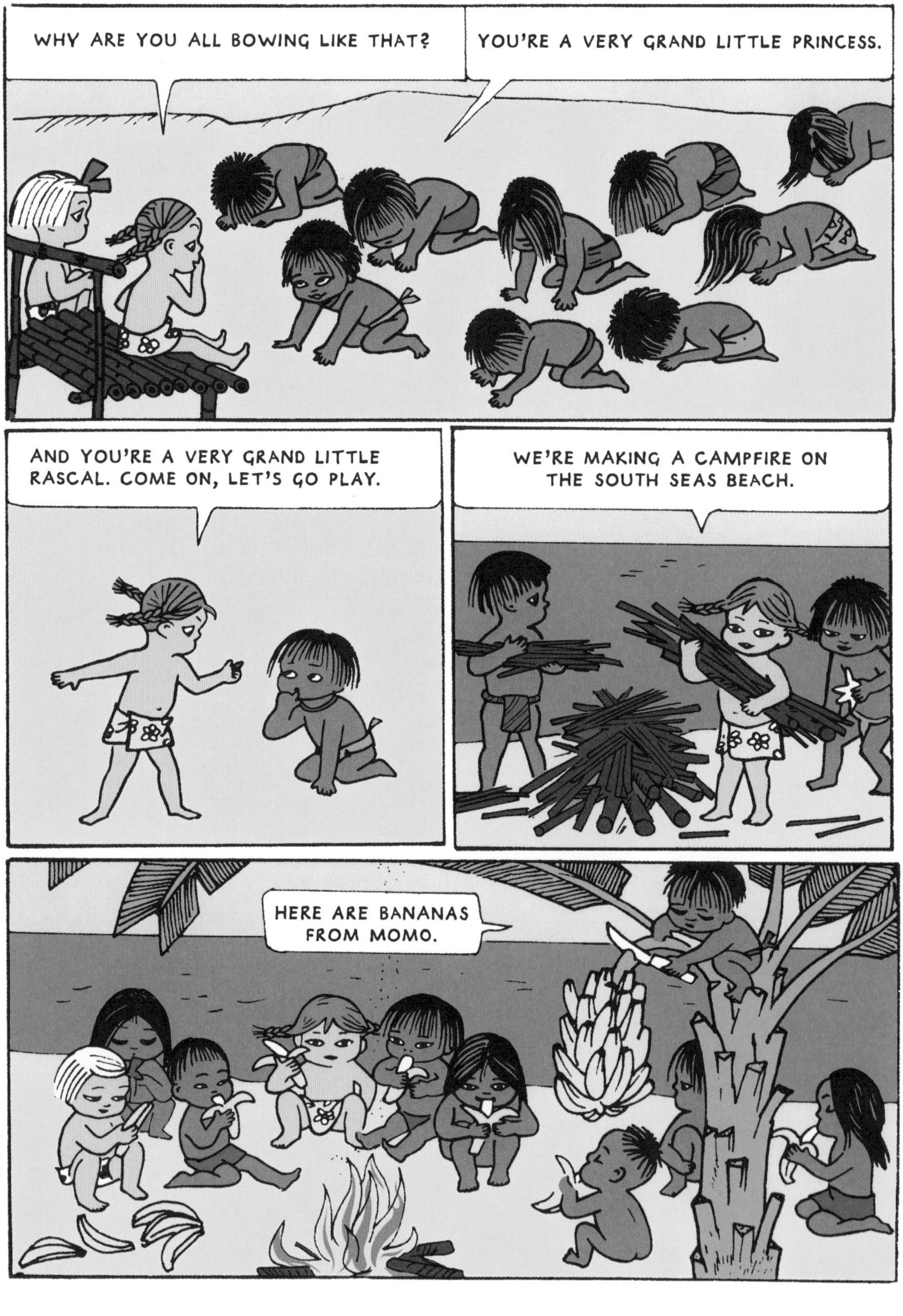
WHY ARE YOU ALL BOWING LIKE THAT?
YOU'RE A VERY GRAND LITTLE PRINCESS.
AND YOU'RE A VERY GRAND LITTLE RASCAL. COME ON, LET'S GO PLAY.
WE'RE MAKING A CAMPFIRE ON THE SOUTH SEAS BEACH.
HERE ARE BANANAS FROM MOMO.

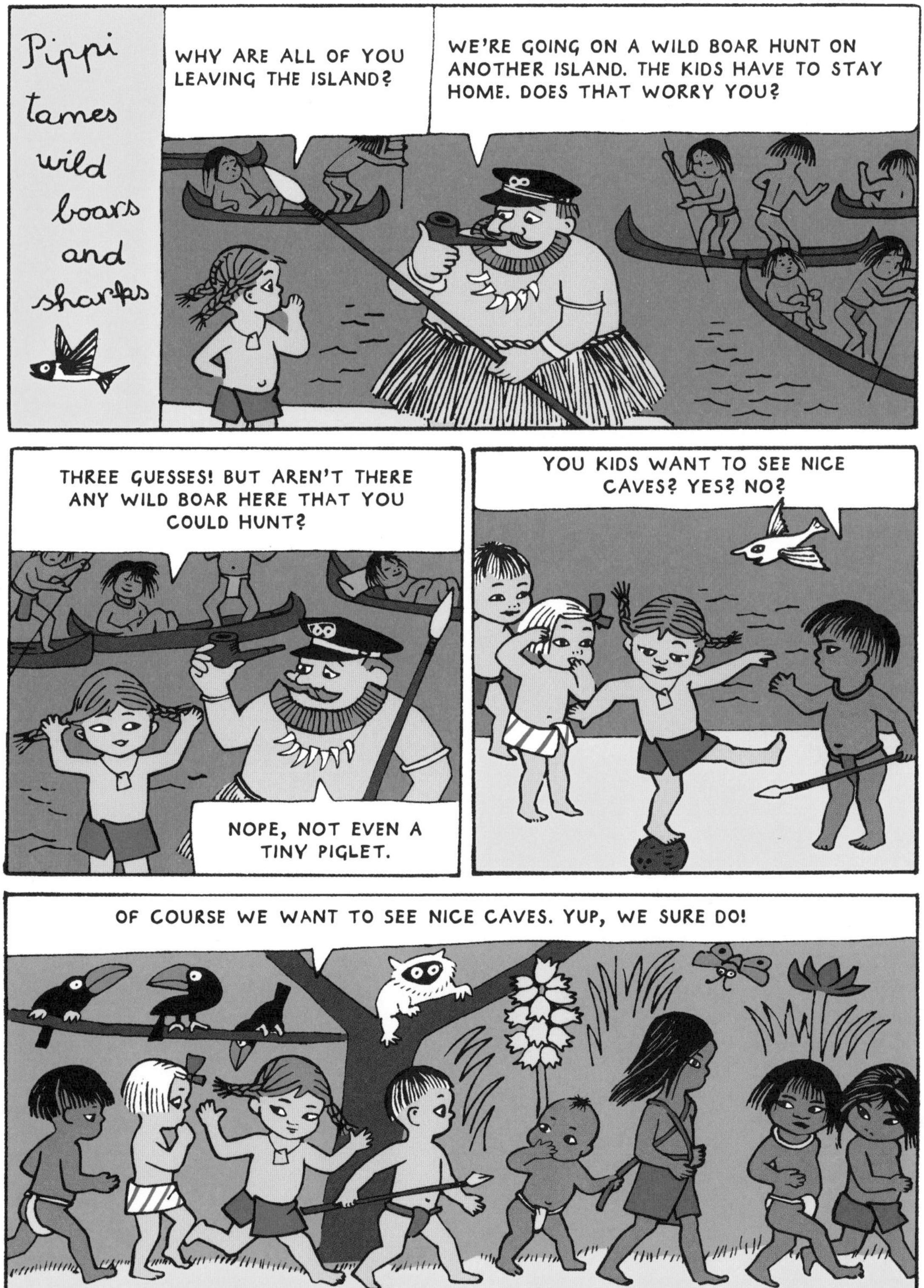
Pippi tames wild boars and sharks
WHY ARE ALL OF YOU LEAVING THE ISLAND?
WE'RE GOING ON A WILD BOAR HUNT ON ANOTHER ISLAND. THE KIDS HAVE TO STAY HOME. DOES THAT WORRY YOU?
THREE GUESSES! BUT AREN'T THERE ANY WILD BOAR HERE THAT YOU COULD HUNT?
NOPE, NOT EVEN A TINY PIGLET.
YOU KIDS WANT TO SEE NICE CAVES? YES? NO?
OF COURSE WE WANT TO SEE NICE CAVES. YUP, WE SURE DO!

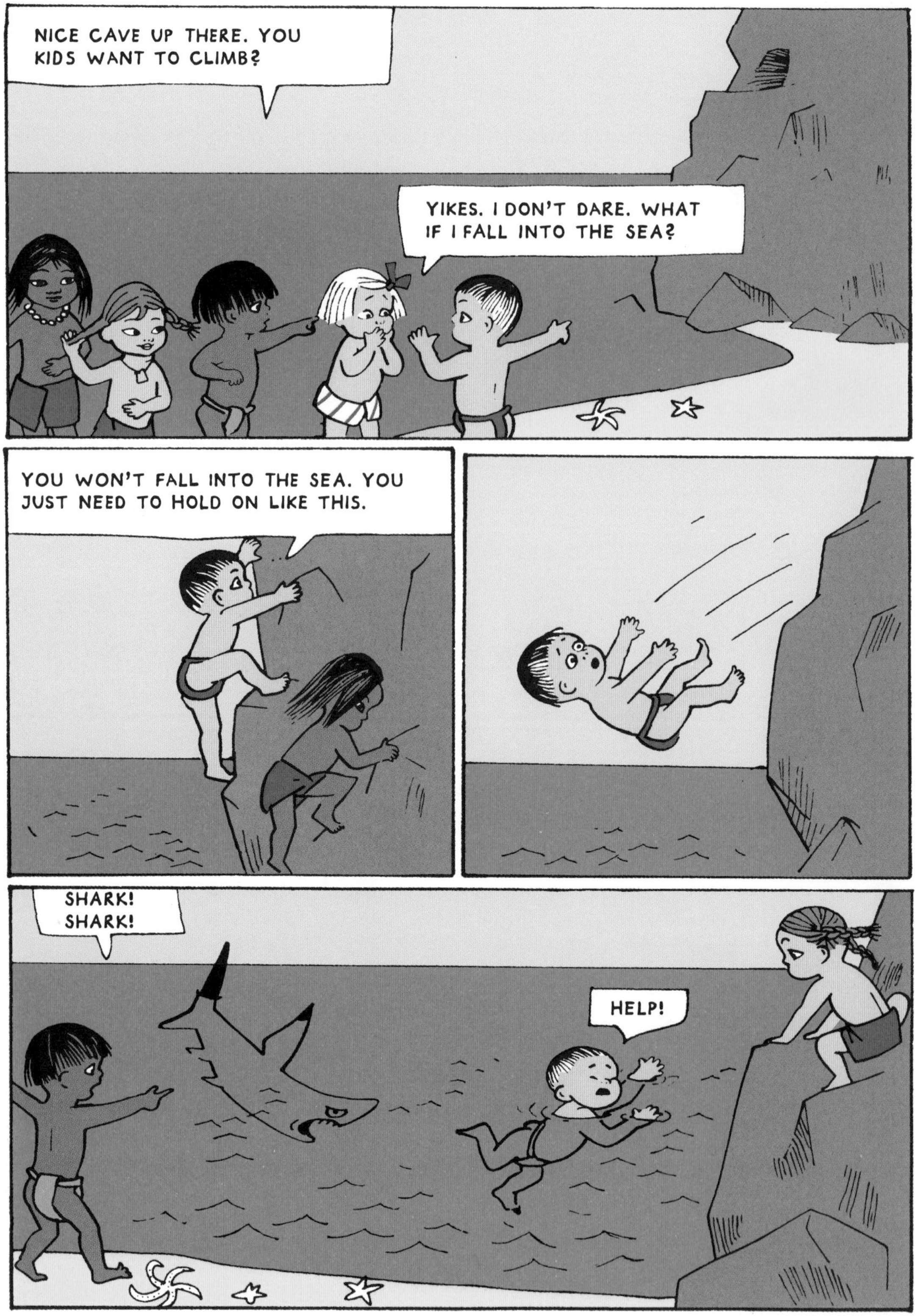
NICE CAVE UP THERE. YOU KIDS WANT TO CLIMB?
YIKES. I DON'T DARE. WHAT IF I FALL INTO THE SEA?
YOU WON'T FALL INTO THE SEA. YOU JUST NEED TO HOLD ON LIKE THIS.
SHARK! SHARK!
HELP!

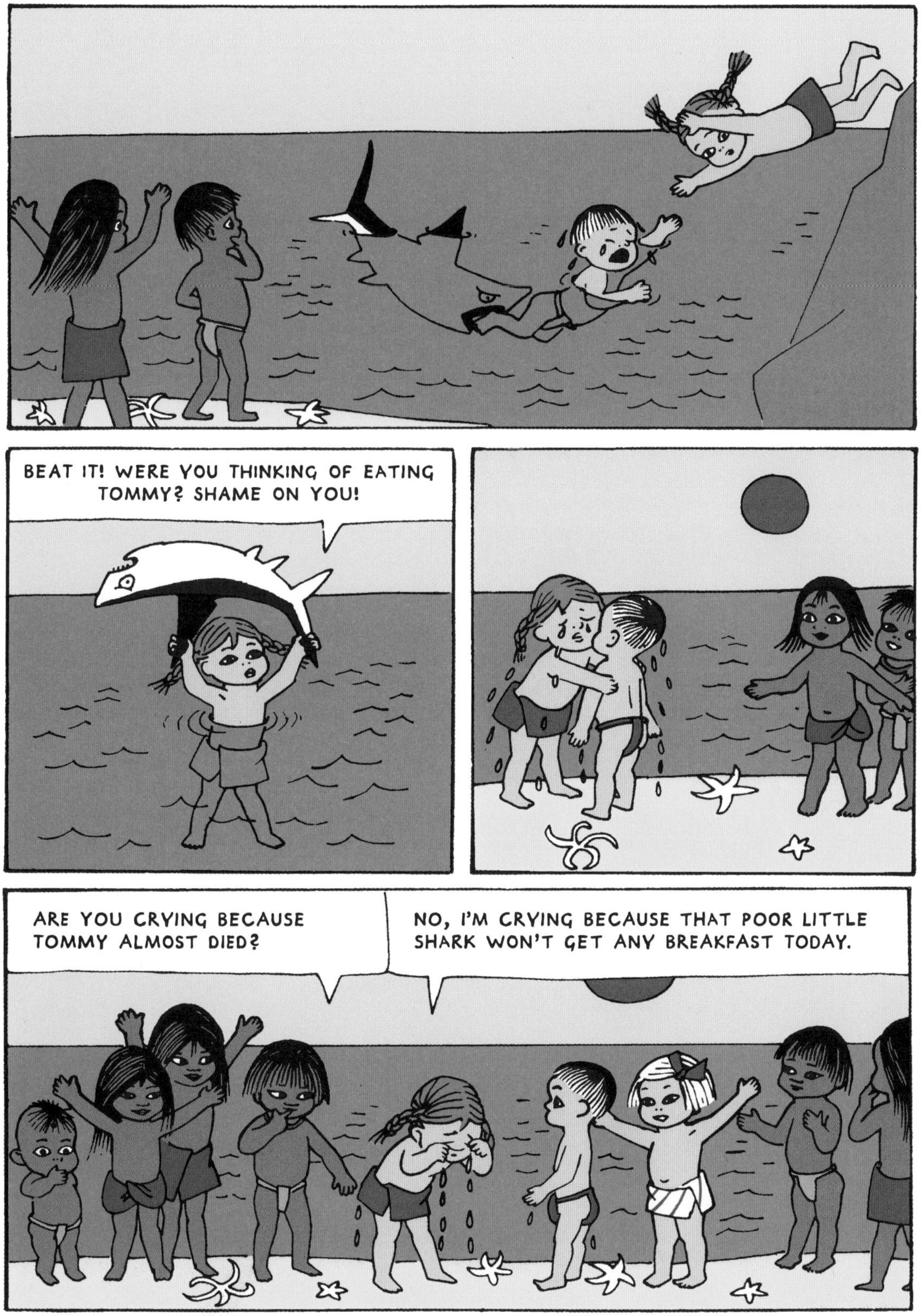
BEAT IT! WERE YOU THINKING OF EATING TOMMY? SHAME ON YOU!
ARE YOU CRYING BECAUSE TOMMY ALMOST DIED?
NO, I'M CRYING BECAUSE THAT POOR LITTLE SHARK WON'T GET ANY BREAKFAST TODAY.

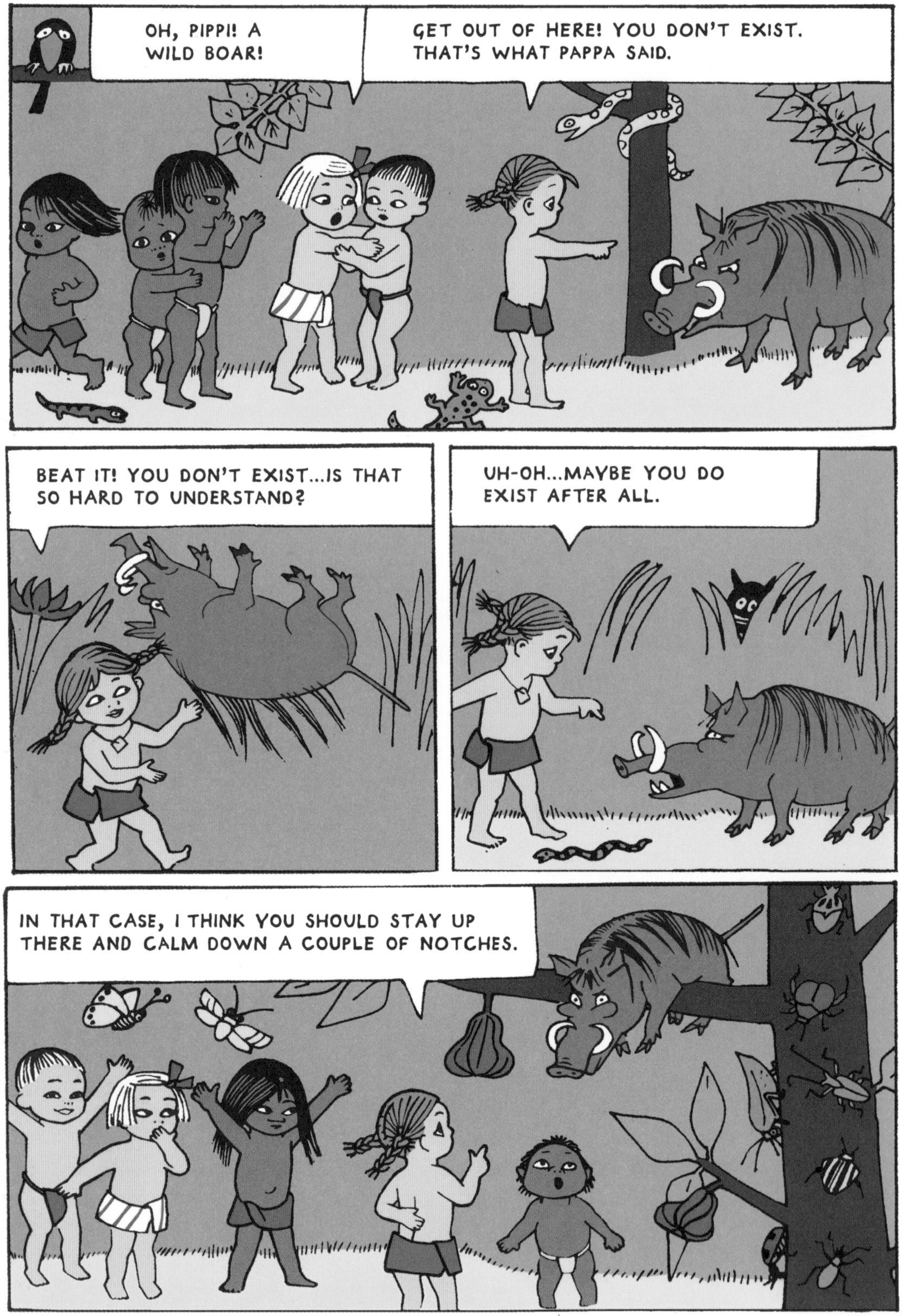
OH, PIPPI! A WILD BOAR!
GET OUT OF HERE! YOU DON'T EXIST. THAT'S WHAT PAPPA SAID.
BEAT IT! YOU DON'T EXIST...IS THAT SO HARD TO UNDERSTAND?
UH-OH...MAYBE YOU DO EXIST AFTER ALL.
IN THAT CASE, I THINK YOU SHOULD STAY UP THERE AND CALM DOWN A COUPLE OF NOTCHES.

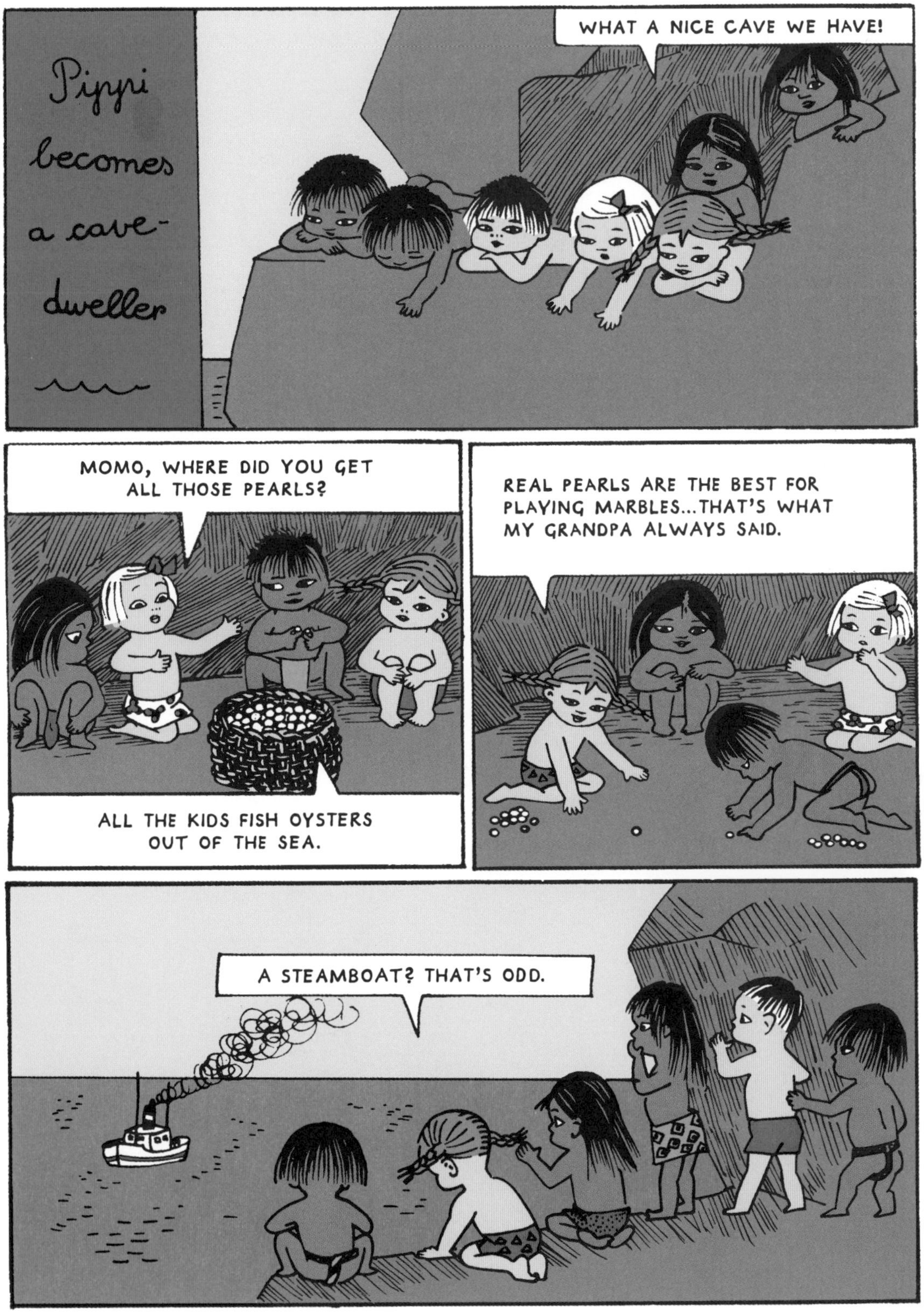
Pippi becomes a cave-dweller
WHAT A NICE CAVE WE HAVE!
MOMO, WHERE DID YOU GET ALL THOSE PEARLS?
ALL THE KIDS FISH OYSTERS OUT OF THE SEA.
REAL PEARLS ARE THE BEST FOR PLAYING MARBLES...THAT'S WHAT MY GRANDPA ALWAYS SAID.
A STEAMBOAT? THAT'S ODD.

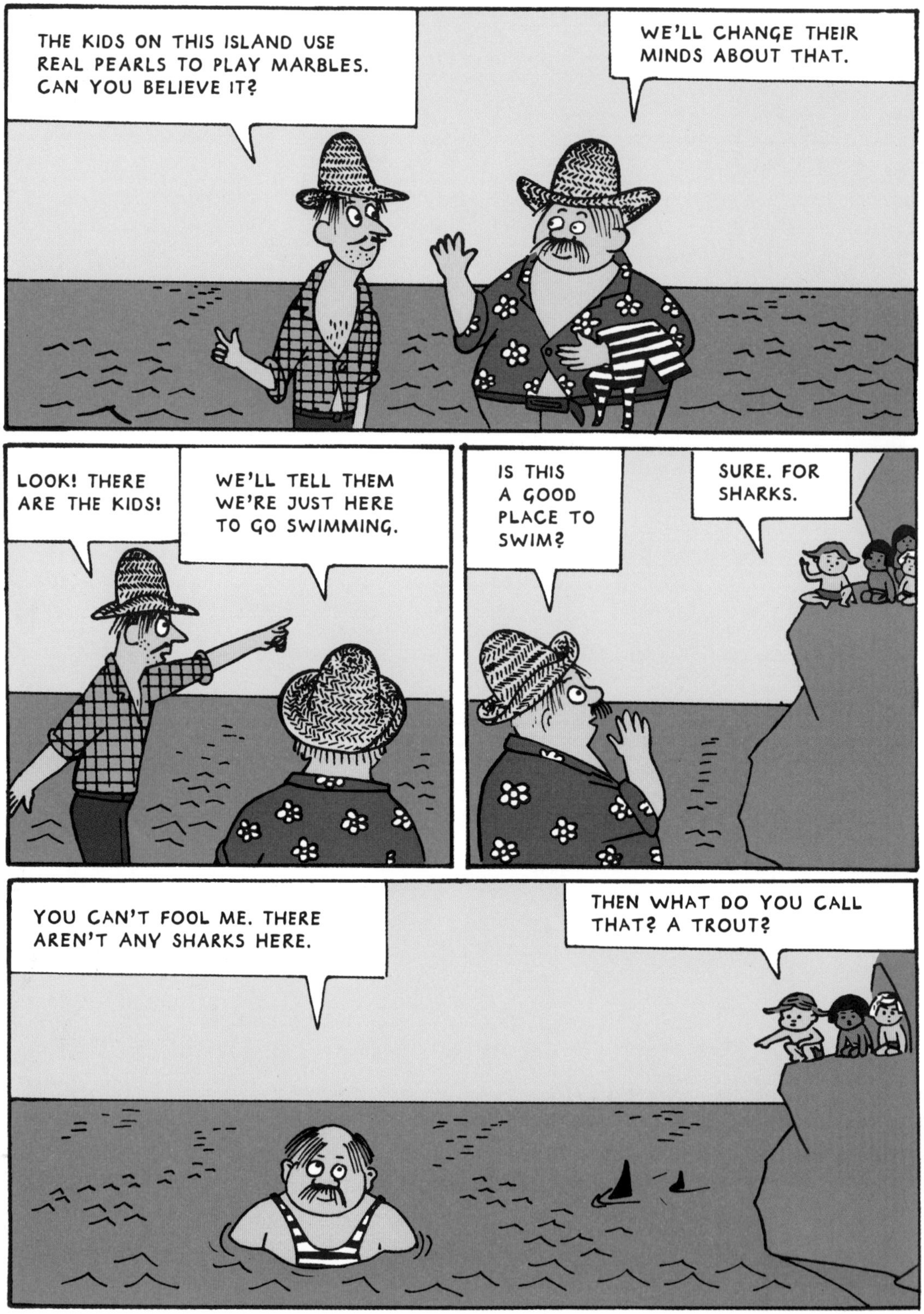
THE KIDS ON THIS ISLAND USE REAL PEARLS TO PLAY MARBLES. CAN YOU BELIEVE IT?
WE'LL CHANGE THEIR MINDS ABOUT THAT.
LOOK! THERE ARE THE KIDS!
WE'LL TELL THEM WE'RE JUST HERE TO GO SWIMMING.
IS THIS A GOOD PLACE TO SWIM?
SURE. FOR SHARKS.
YOU CAN'T FOOL ME. THERE AREN'T ANY SHARKS HERE.
THEN WHAT DO YOU CALL THAT? A TROUT?

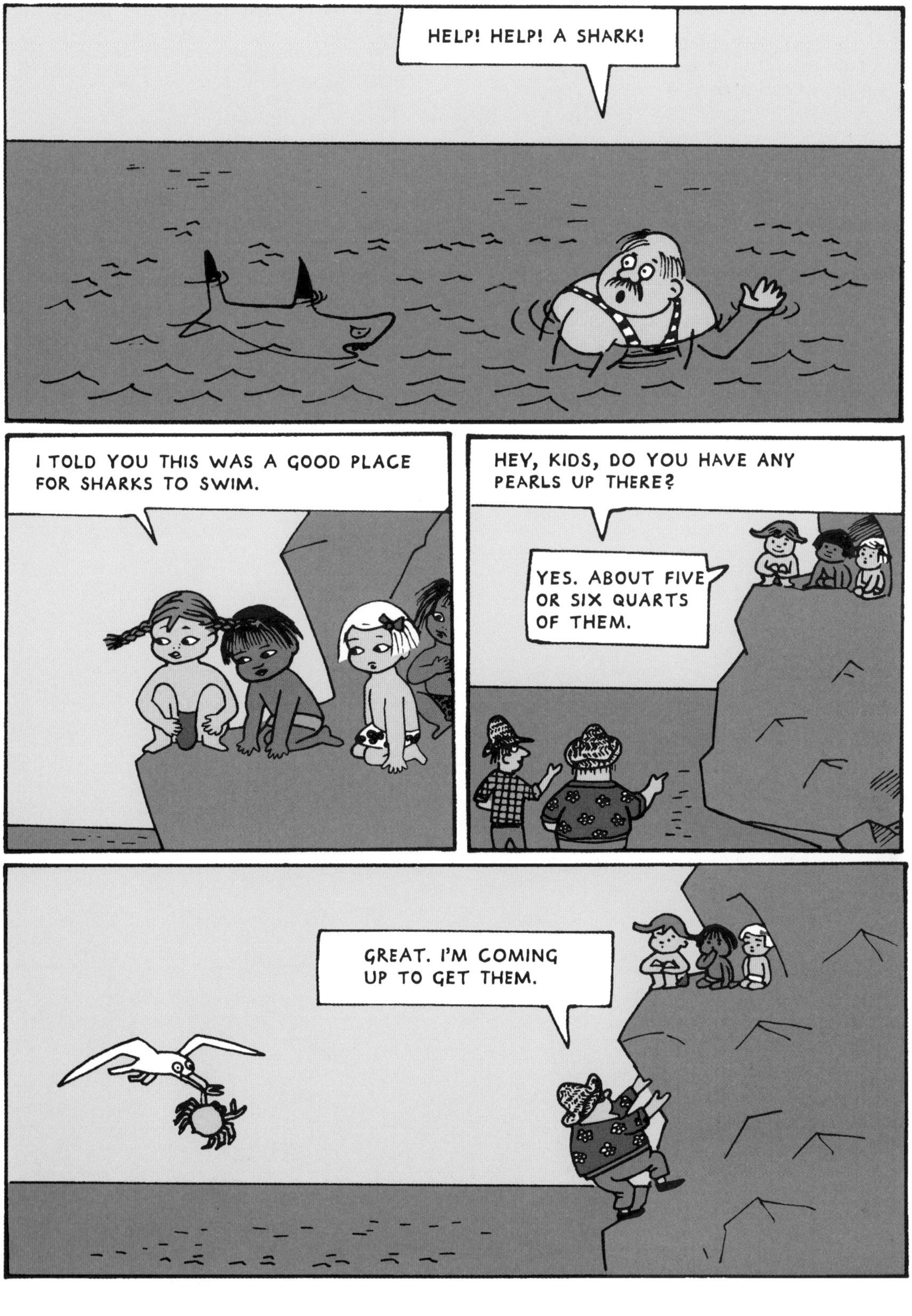
HELP! HELP! A SHARK!
I TOLD YOU THIS WAS A GOOD PLACE FOR SHARKS TO SWIM.
HEY, KIDS, DO YOU HAVE ANY PEARLS UP THERE?
YES. ABOUT FIVE OR SIX QUARTS OF THEM.
GREAT. I'M COMING UP TO GET THEM.

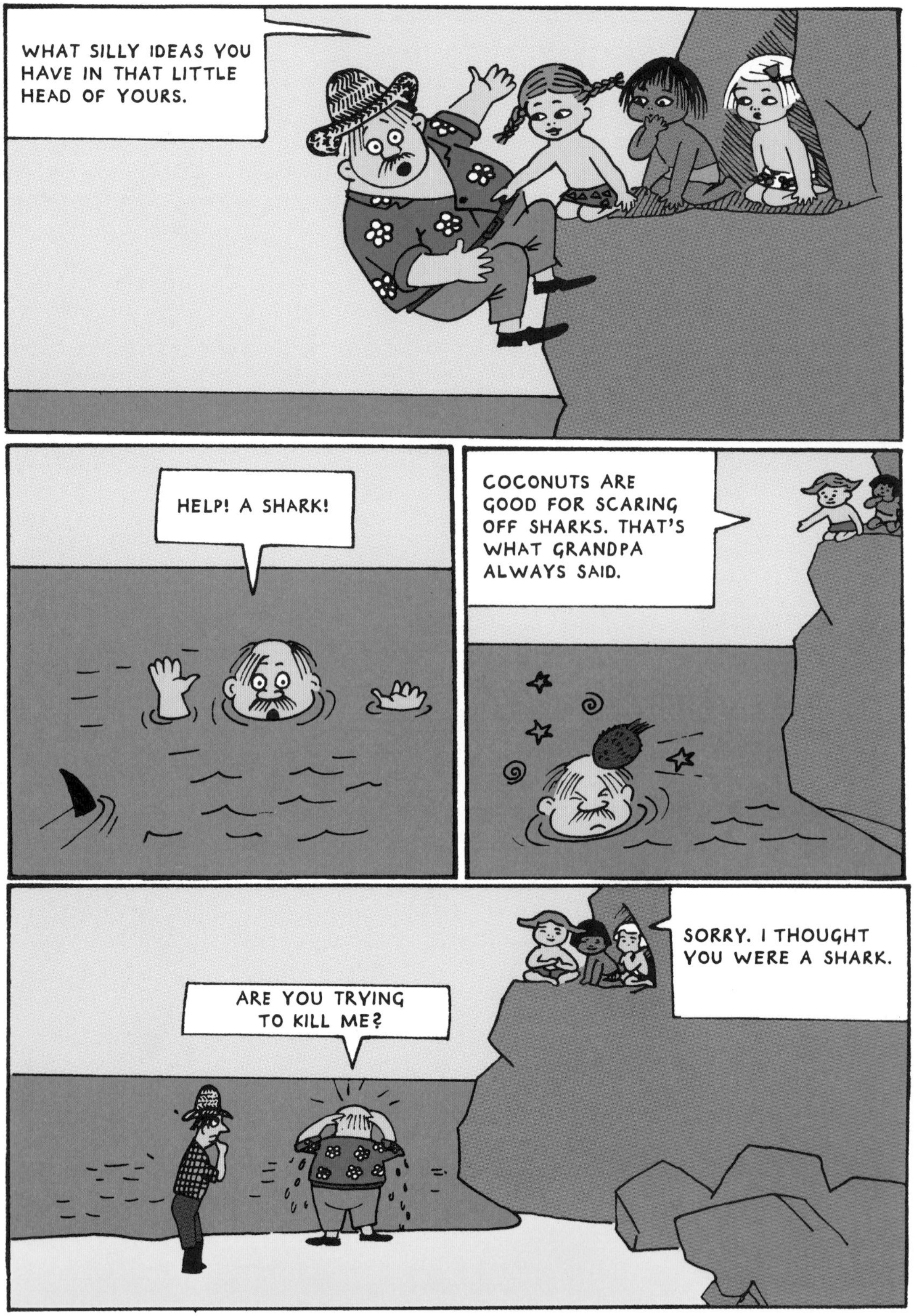
WHAT SILLY IDEAS YOU HAVE IN THAT LITTLE HEAD OF YOURS.
HELP! A SHARK!
COCONUTS ARE GOOD FOR SCARING OFF SHARKS. THAT'S WHAT GRANDPA ALWAYS SAID.
ARE YOU TRYING TO KILL ME?
SORRY. I THOUGHT YOU WERE A SHARK.

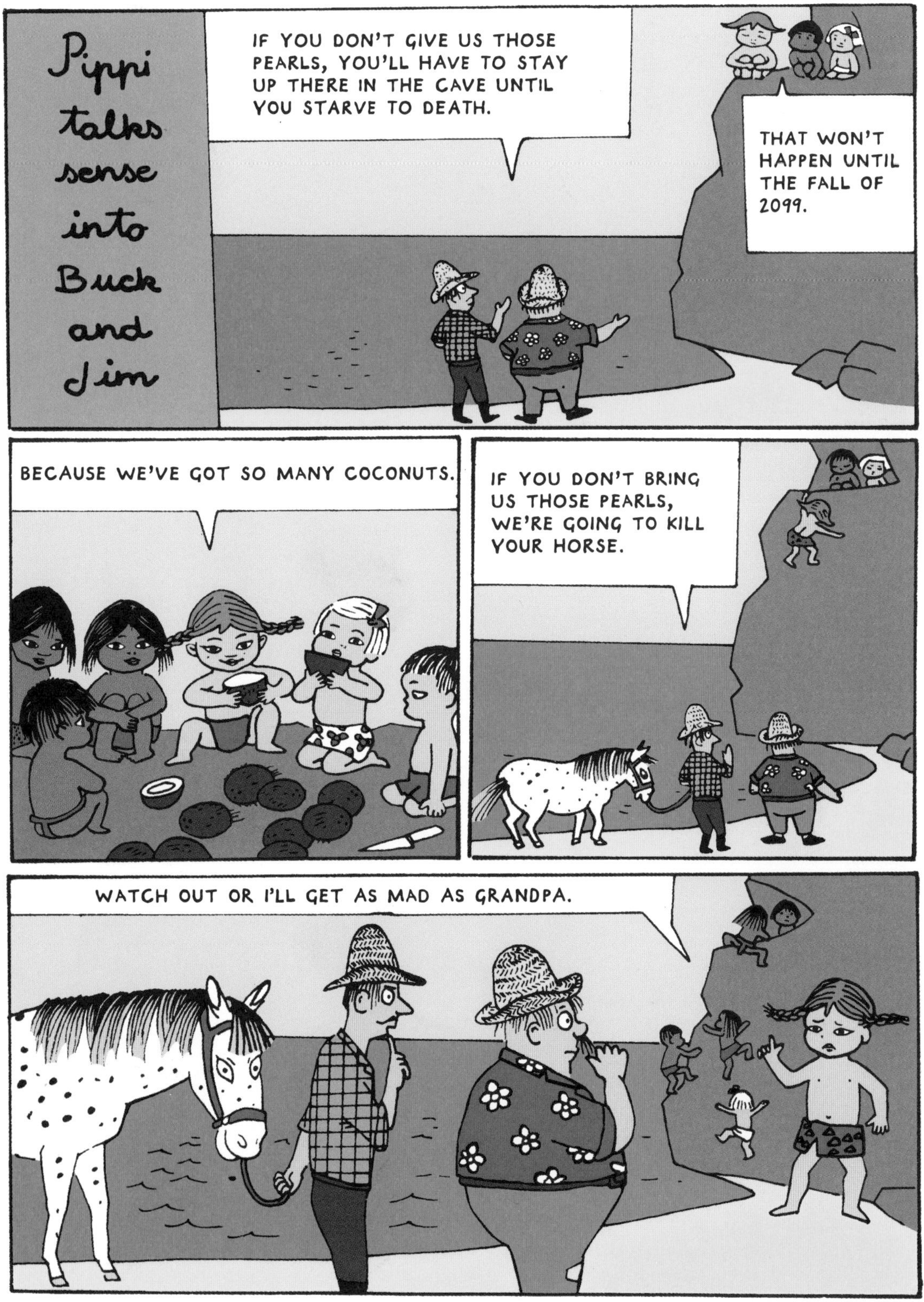
Pippi talks sense into Buck and Jim
IF YOU DON'T GIVE US THOSE PEARLS, YOU'LL HAVE TO STAY UP THERE IN THE CAVE UNTIL YOU STARVE TO DEATH.
THAT WON'T HAPPEN UNTIL THE FALL OF 2099.
BECAUSE WE'VE GOT SO MANY COCONUTS.
IF YOU DON'T BRING US THOSE PEARLS, WE'RE GOING TO KILL YOUR HORSE.
WATCH OUT OR I'LL GET AS MAD AS GRANDPA.

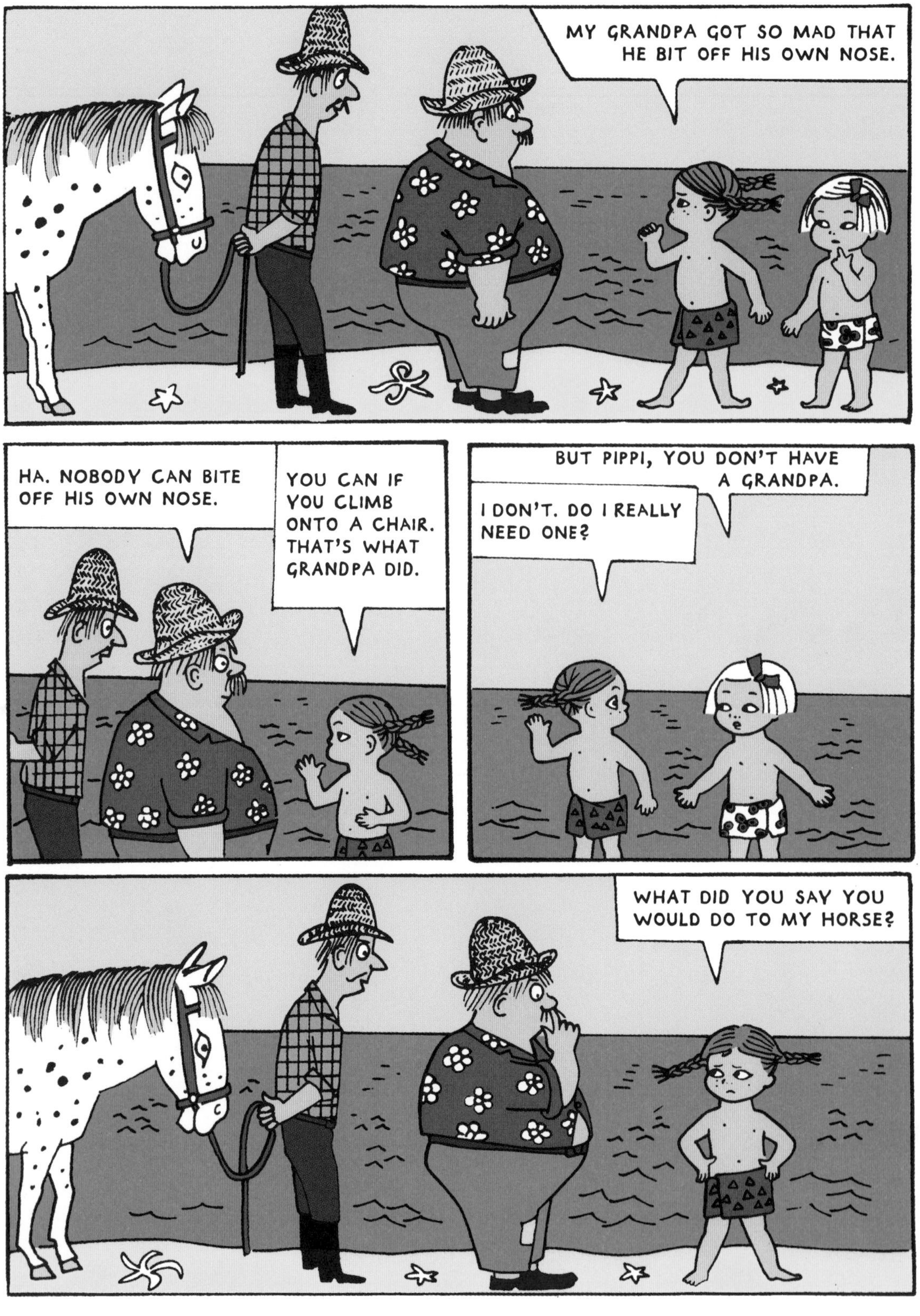
MY GRANDPA GOT SO MAD THAT HE BIT OFF HIS OWN NOSE.
HA. NOBODY CAN BITE OFF HIS OWN NOSE.
YOU CAN IF YOU CLIMB ONTO A CHAIR. THAT'S WHAT GRANDPA DID.
BUT PIPPI, YOU DON'T HAVE A GRANDPA.
I DON'T. DO I REALLY NEED ONE?
WHAT DID YOU SAY YOU WOULD DO TO MY HORSE?

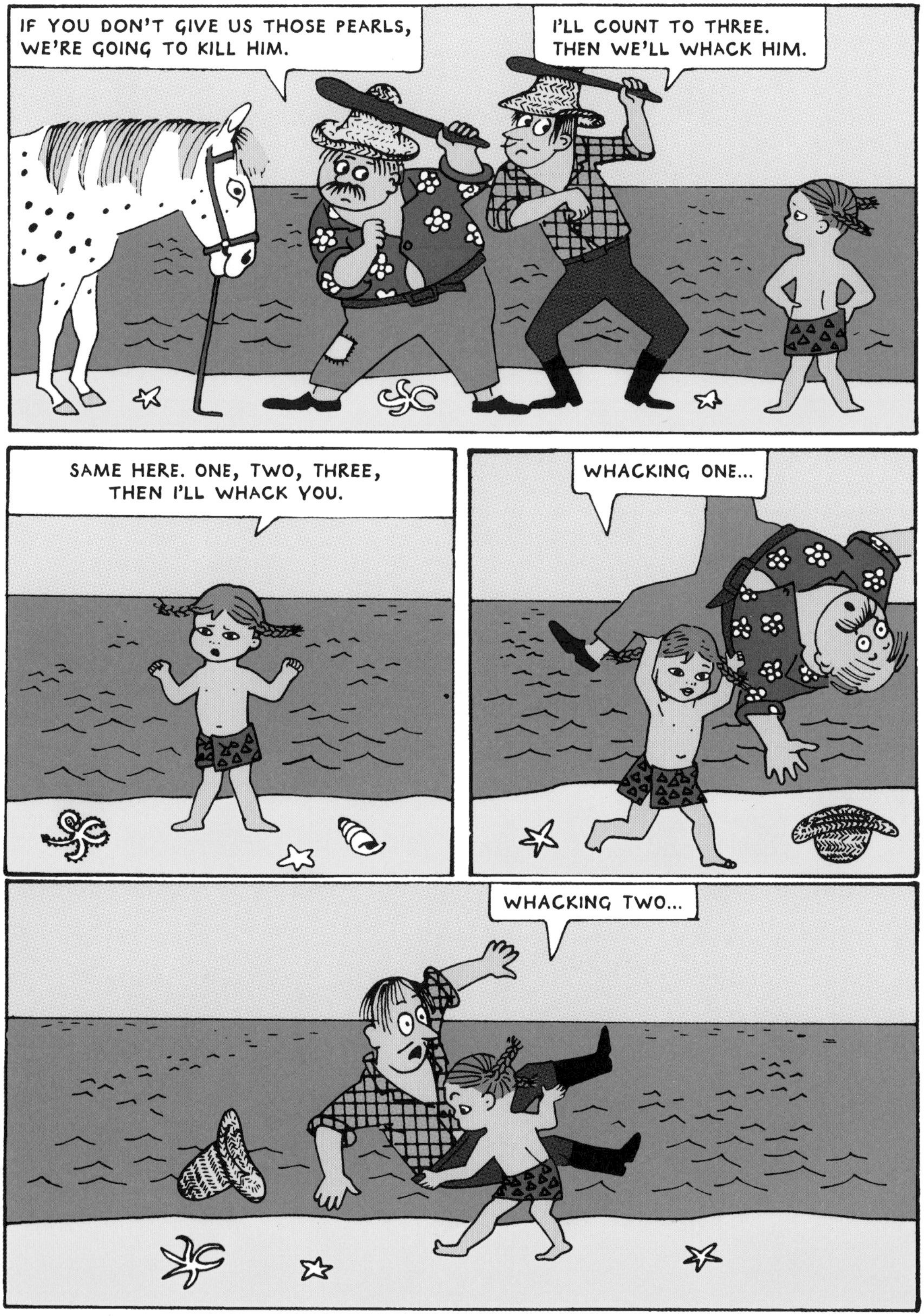
IF YOU DON'T GIVE US THOSE PEARLS, WE'RE GOING TO KILL HIM.
I'LL COUNT TO THREE. THEN WE'LL WHACK HIM.
SAME HERE. ONE, TWO, THREE, THEN I'LL WHACK YOU.
WHACKING ONE...
WHACKING TWO...

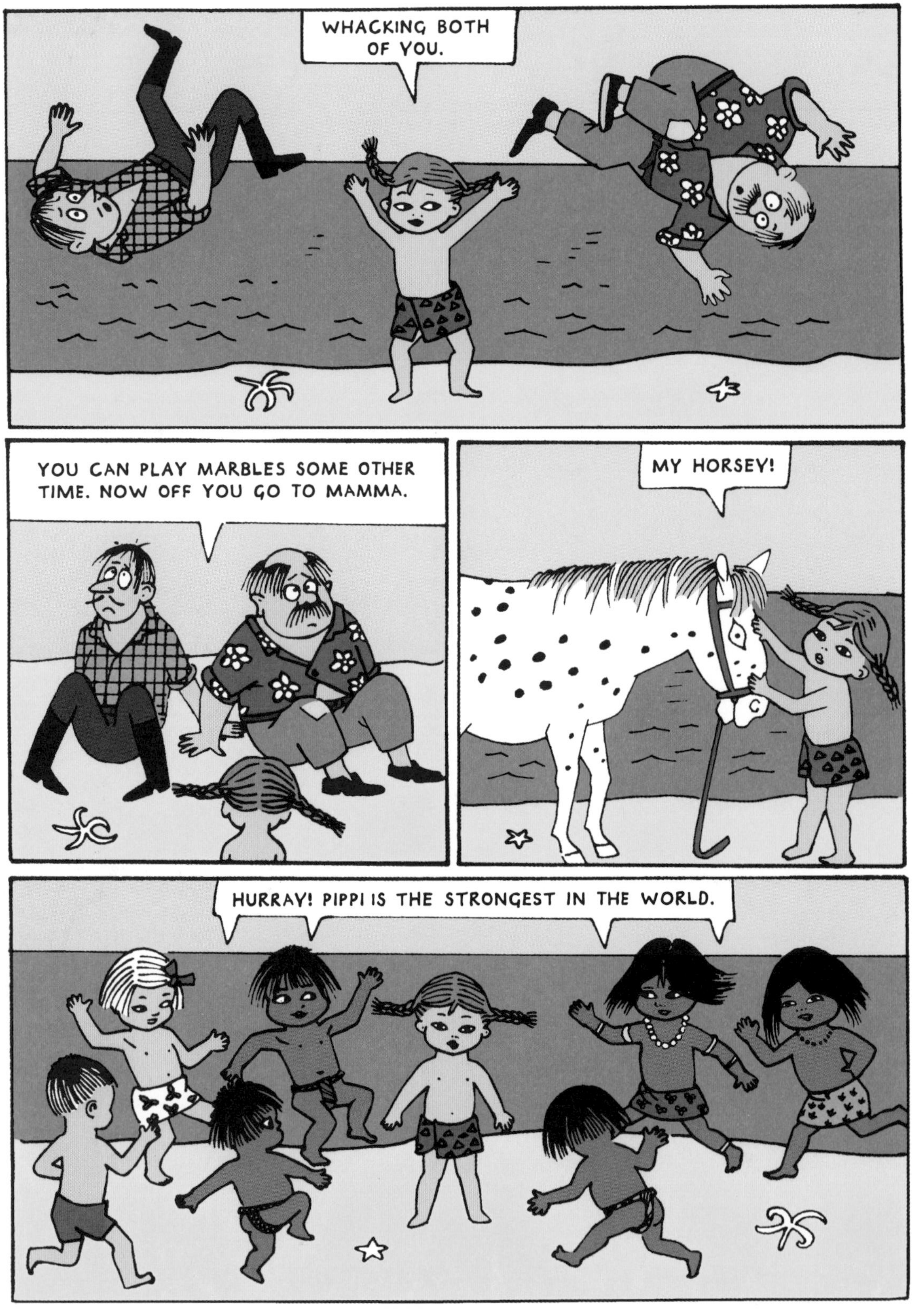
WHACKING BOTH OF YOU.
YOU CAN PLAY MARBLES SOME OTHER TIME. NOW OFF YOU GO TO MAMMA.
MY HORSEY!
HURRAY! PIPPI IS THE STRONGEST IN THE WORLD.

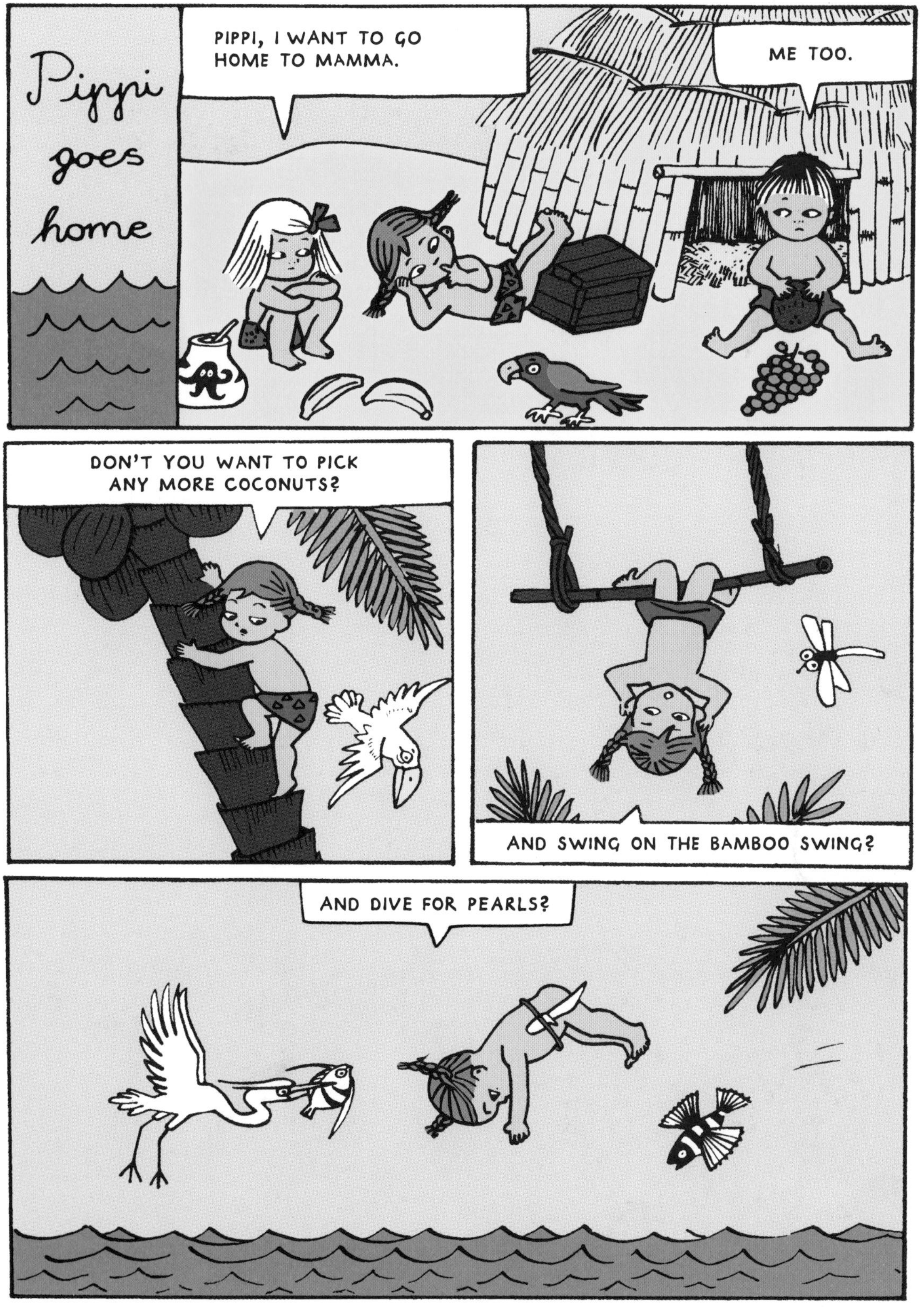
Pippi goes home
PIPPI, I WANT TO GO HOME TO MAMMA.
ME TOO.
DON'T YOU WANT TO PICK ANY MORE COCONUTS?
AND SWING ON THE BAMBOO SWING?
AND DIVE FOR PEARLS?

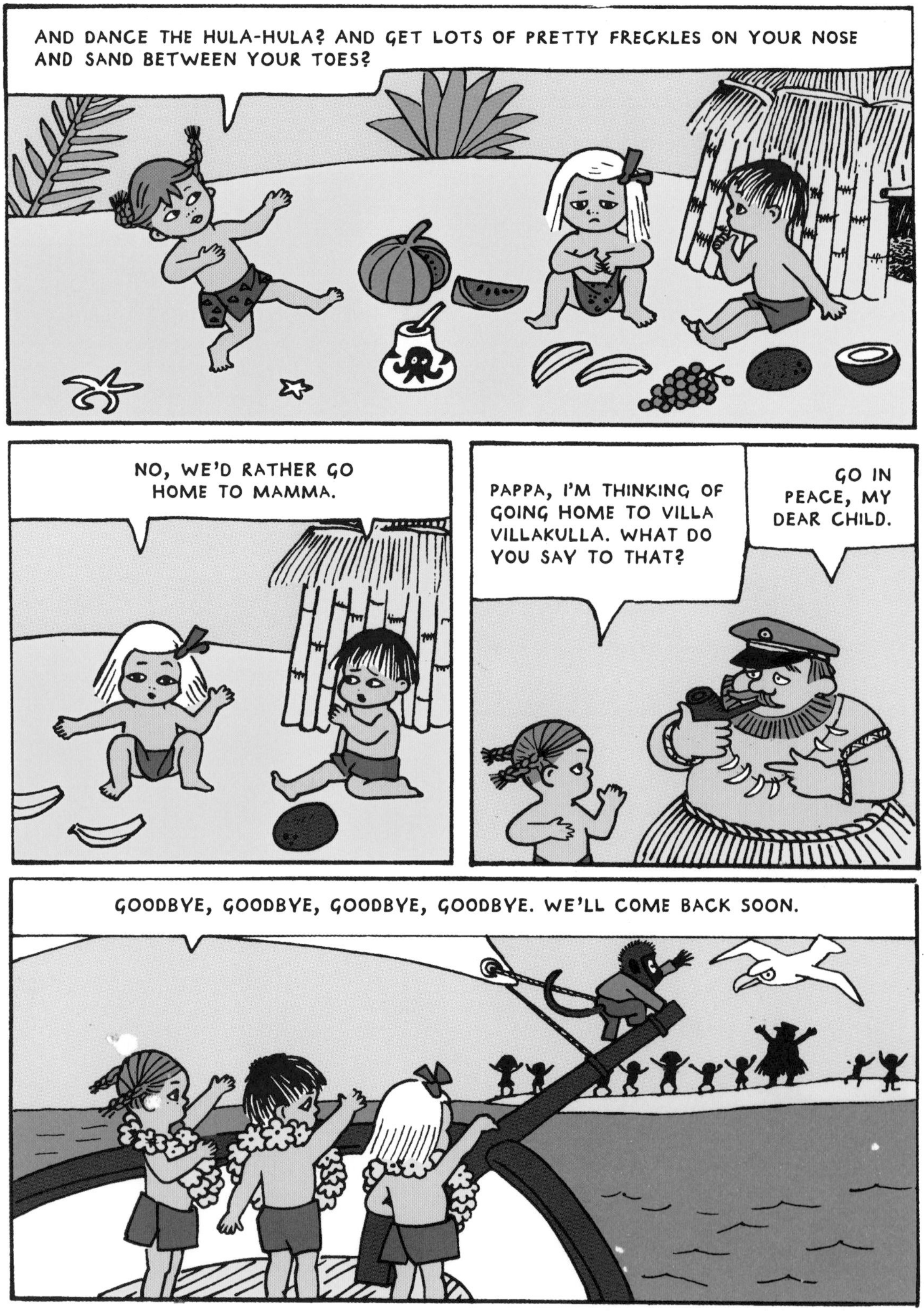
AND DANCE THE HULA-HULA? AND GET LOTS OF PRETTY FRECKLES ON YOUR NOSE AND SAND BETWEEN YOUR TOES?
NO, WE'D RATHER GO HOME TO MAMMA.
PAPPA, I'M THINKING OF GOING HOME TO VILLA VILLAKULLA. WHAT DO YOU SAY TO THAT?
GO IN PEACE, MY DEAR CHILD.
GOODBYE, GOODBYE, GOODBYE, GOODBYE. WE'LL COME BACK SOON.

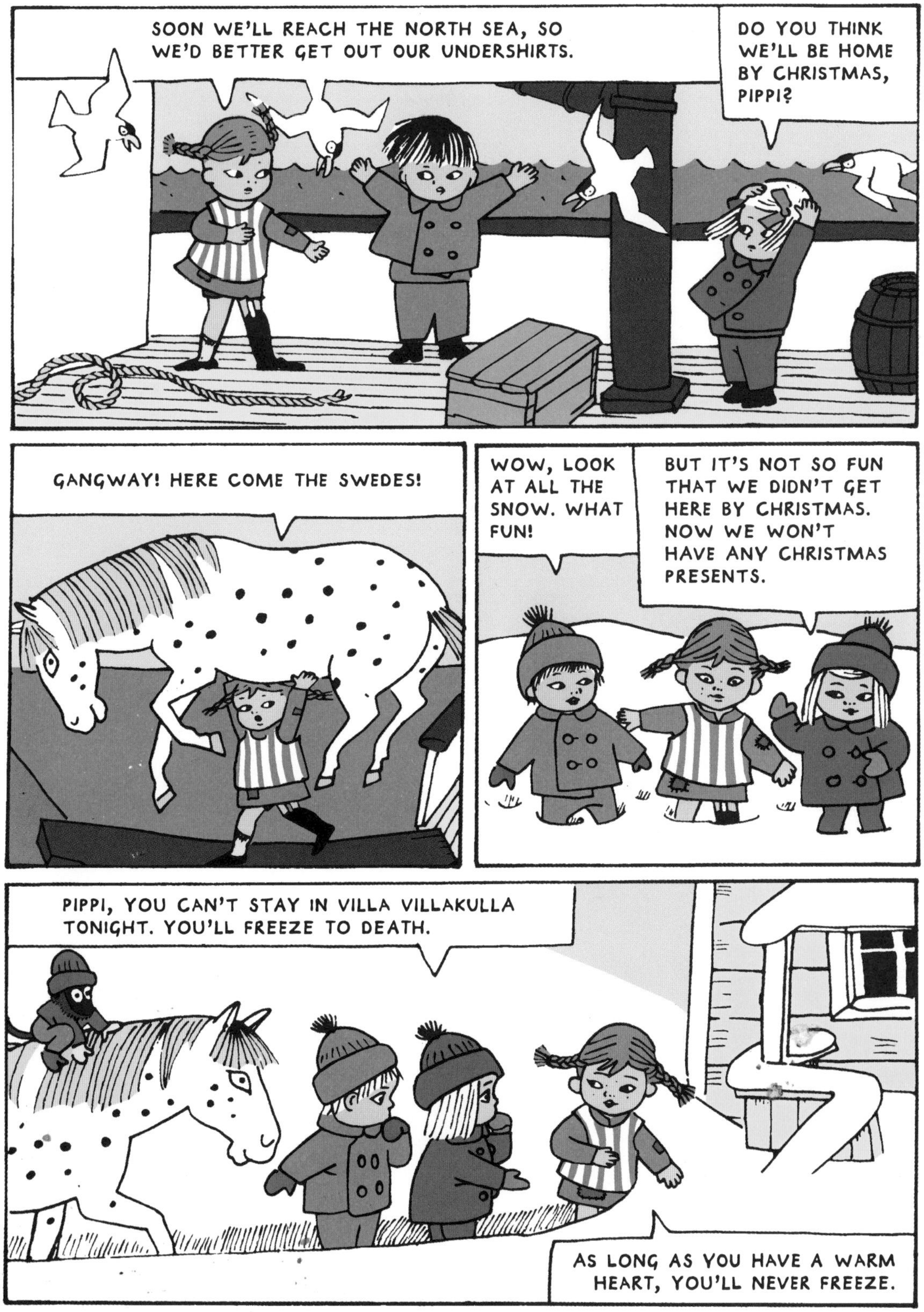
SOON WE'LL REACH THE NORTH SEA, SO WE'D BETTER GET OUT OUR UNDERSHIRTS.
DO YOU THINK WE'LL BE HOME BY CHRISTMAS, PIPPI?
GANGWAY! HERE COME THE SWEDES!
WOW, LOOK AT ALL THE SNOW. WHAT FUN!
BUT IT'S NOT SO FUN THAT WE DIDN'T GET HERE BY CHRISTMAS. NOW WE WON'T HAVE ANY CHRISTMAS PRESENTS.
PIPPI, YOU CAN'T STAY IN VILLA VILLAKULLA TONIGHT. YOU'LL FREEZE TO DEATH.
AS LONG AS YOU HAVE A WARM HEART, YOU'LL NEVER FREEZE.

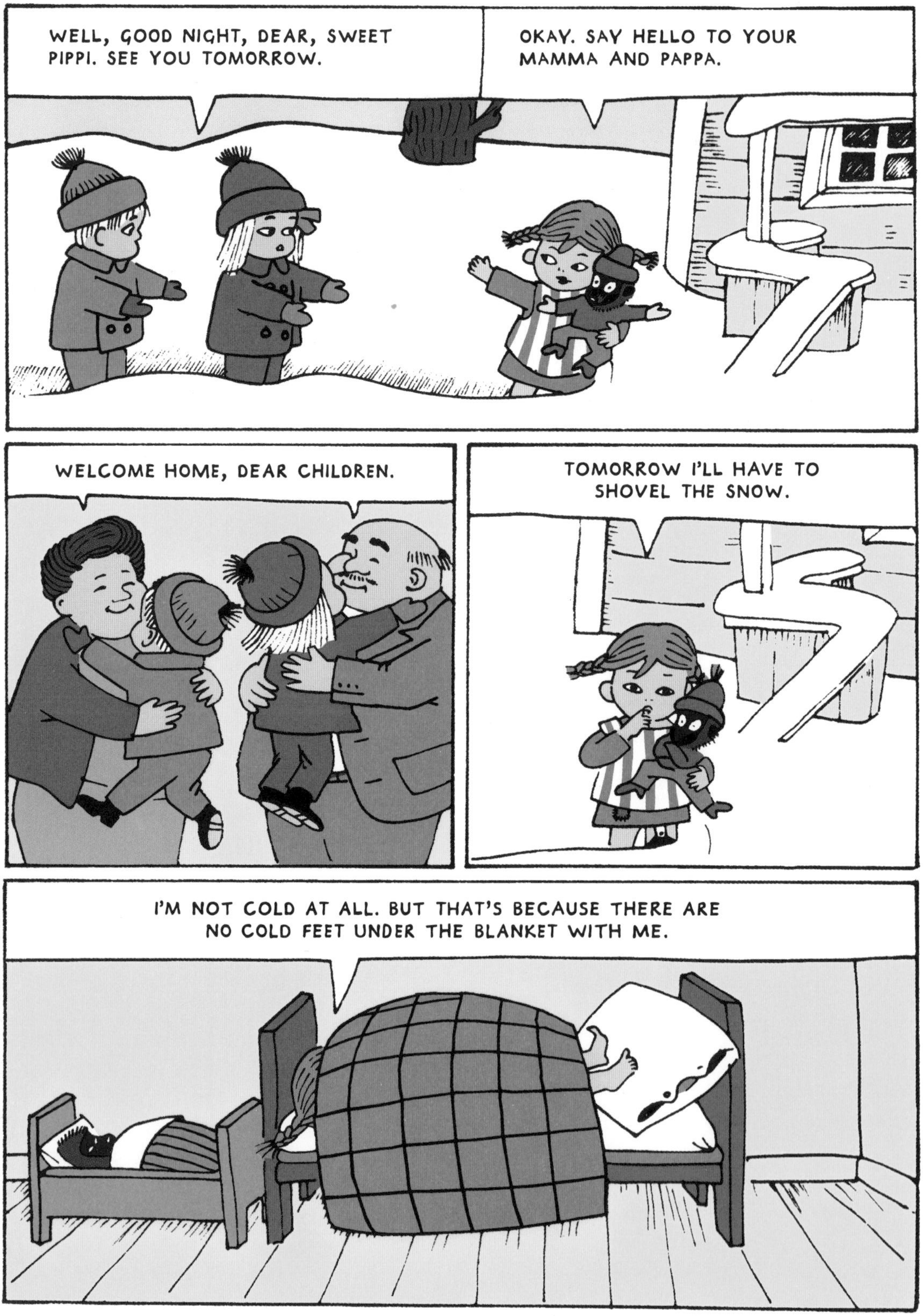
WELL, GOOD NIGHT, DEAR, SWEET PIPPI. SEE YOU TOMORROW.
OKAY. SAY HELLO TO YOUR MAMMA AND PAPPA.
WELCOME HOME, DEAR CHILDREN.
TOMORROW I'LL HAVE TO SHOVEL THE SNOW.
I'M NOT COLD AT ALL. BUT THAT'S BECAUSE THERE ARE NO COLD FEET UNDER THE BLANKET WITH ME.

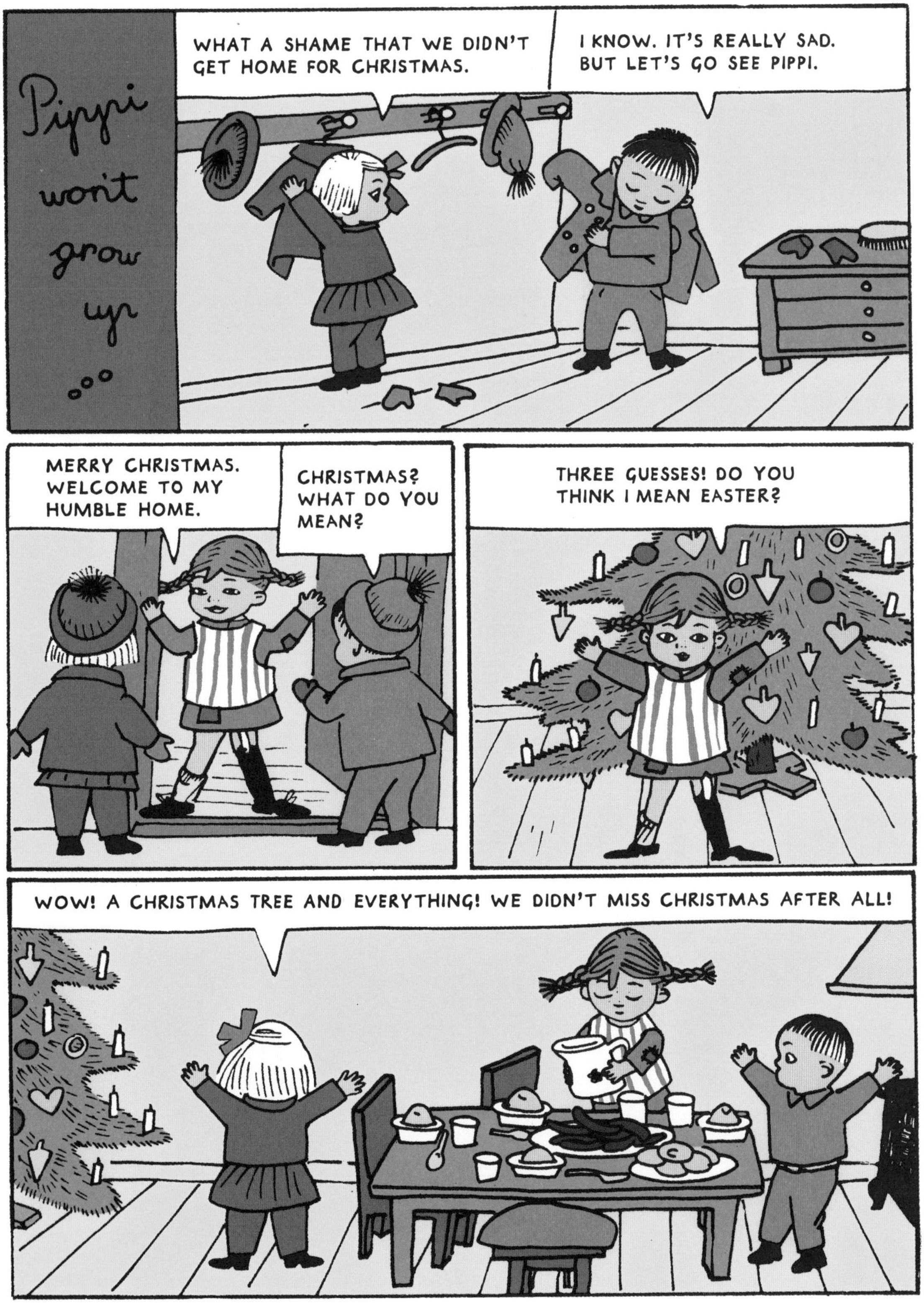
Pippi won't grow up ...
WHAT A SHAME THAT WE DIDN'T GET HOME FOR CHRISTMAS.
I KNOW. IT'S REALLY SAD. BUT LET'S GO SEE PIPPI.
MERRY CHRISTMAS. WELCOME TO MY HUMBLE HOME.
CHRISTMAS? WHAT DO YOU MEAN?
THREE GUESSES! DO YOU THINK I MEAN EASTER?
WOW! A CHRISTMAS TREE AND EVERYTHING! WE DIDN'T MISS CHRISTMAS AFTER ALL!

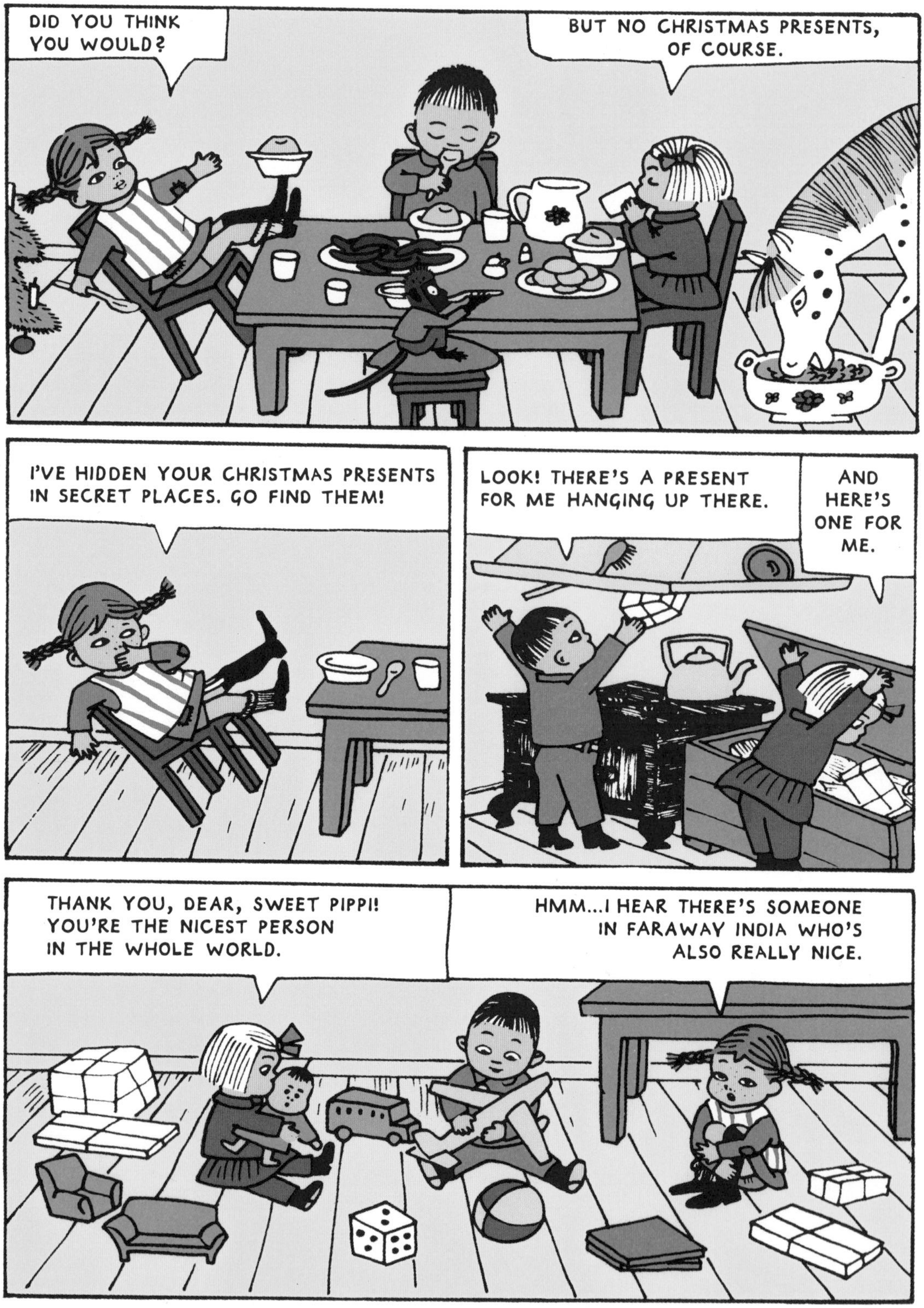
DID YOU THINK YOU WOULD?
BUT NO CHRISTMAS PRESENTS, OF COURSE.
I'VE HIDDEN YOUR CHRISTMAS PRESENTS IN SECRET PLACES. GO FIND THEM!
LOOK! THERE'S A PRESENT FOR ME HANGING UP THERE.
AND HERE'S ONE FOR ME.
THANK YOU, DEAR, SWEET PIPPI! YOU'RE THE NICEST PERSON IN THE WHOLE WORLD.
HMM...I HEAR THERE'S SOMEONE IN FARAWAY INDIA WHO'S ALSO REALLY NICE.

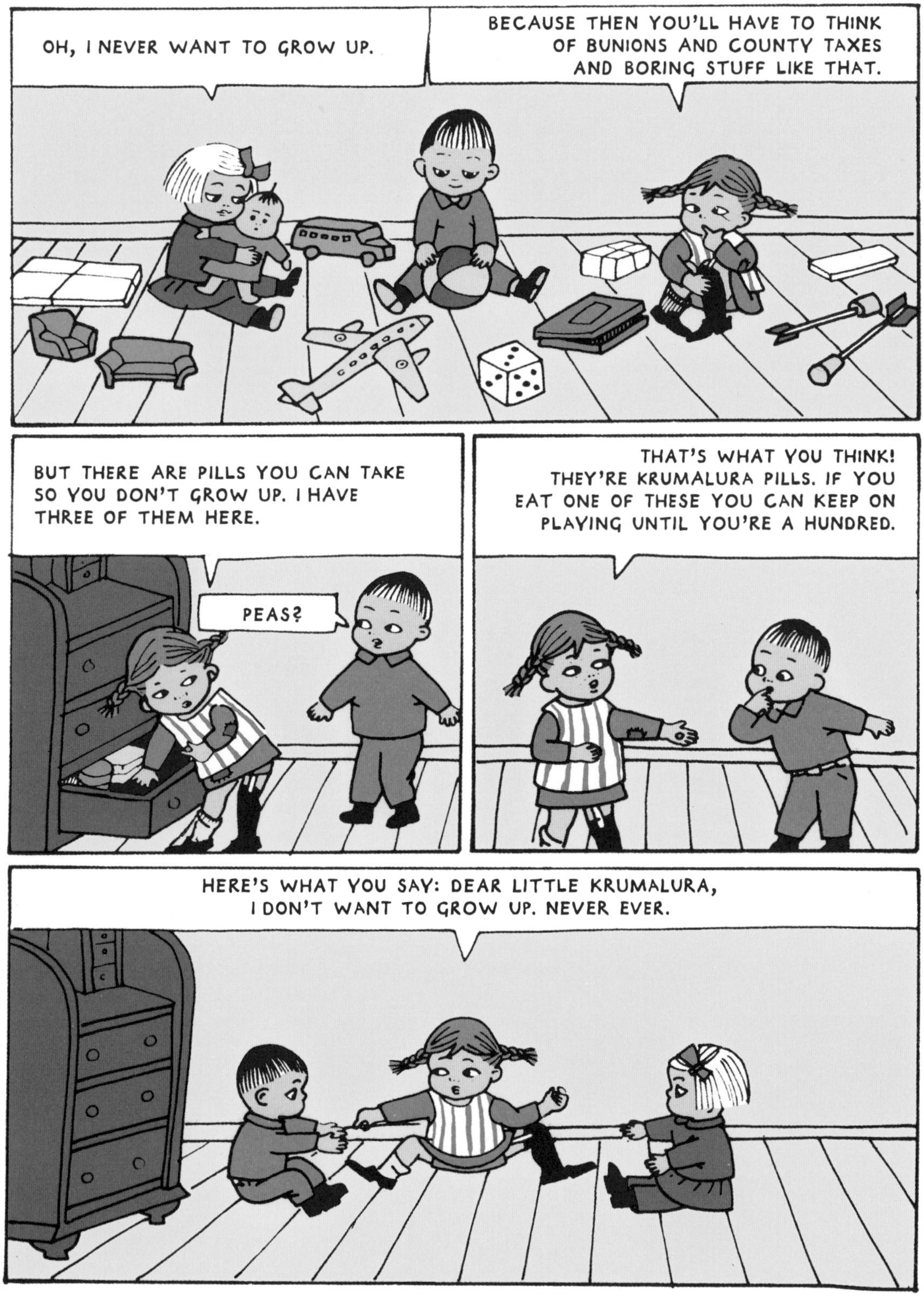
OH, I NEVER WANT TO GROW UP.
BECAUSE THEN YOU'LL HAVE TO THINK OF BUNIONS AND COUNTY TAXES AND BORING STUFF LIKE THAT.
BUT THERE ARE PILLS YOU CAN TAKE SO YOU DON'T GROW UP. I HAVE THREE OF THEM HERE.
PEAS?
THAT'S WHAT YOU THINK! THEY'RE KRUMALURA PILLS. IF YOU EAT ONE OF THESE YOU CAN KEEP ON PLAYING UNTIL YOU'RE A HUNDRED.
HERE'S WHAT YOU SAY: DEAR LITTLE KRUMALURA, I DON'T WANT TO GROW UP. NEVER EVER.

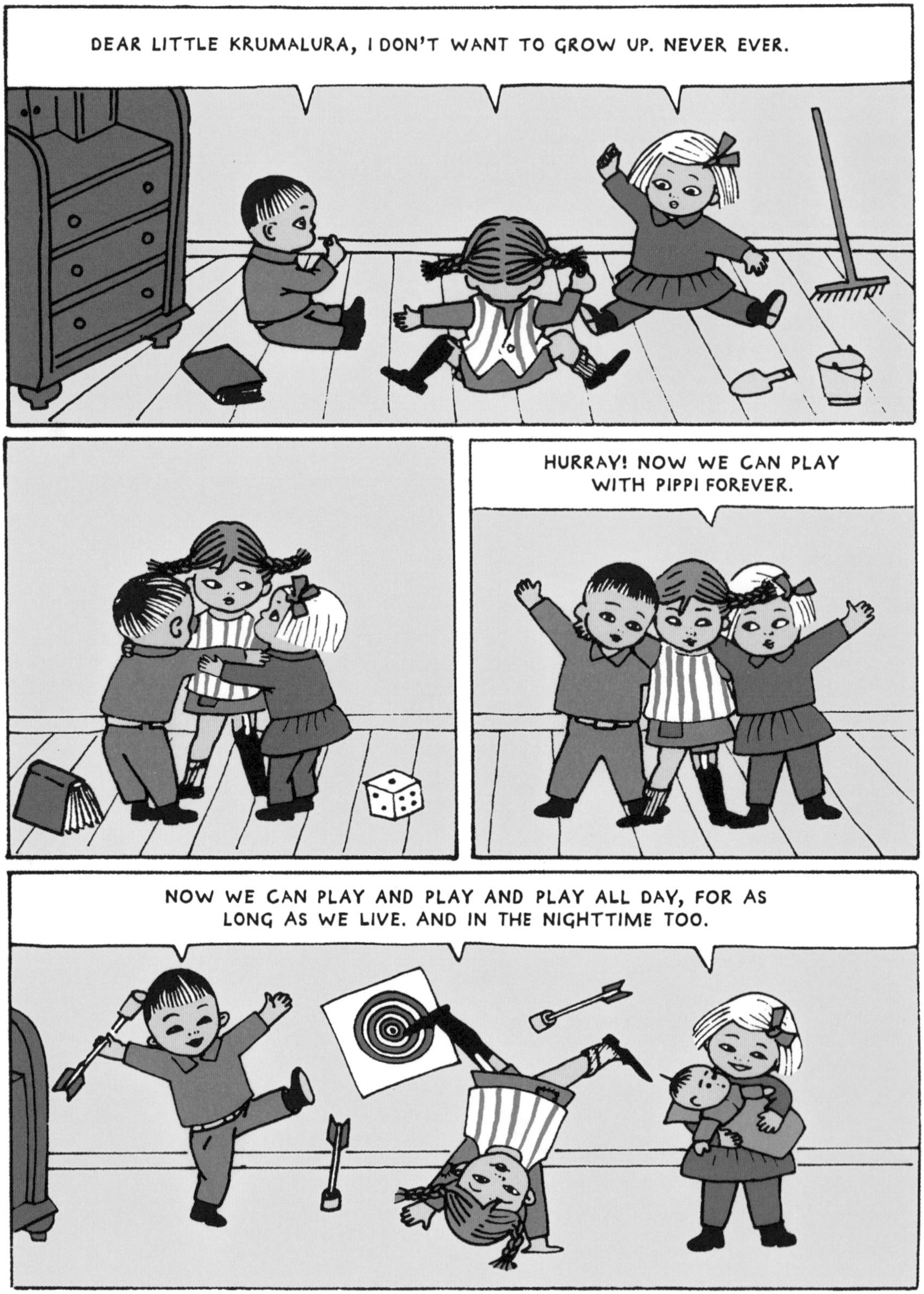
DEAR LITTLE KRUMALURA, I DON'T WANT TO GROW UP. NEVER EVER.
HURRAY! NOW WE CAN PLAY WITH PIPPI FOREVER.
NOW WE CAN PLAY AND PLAY AND PLAY ALL DAY, FOR AS LONG AS WE LIVE. AND IN THE NIGHTTIME TOO.

Astrid Lindgren (1907–2002) was an immensely popular

children's book author as well as a lifelong philanthropist. Her Pippi Longstocking series—*Pippi Longstocking* (1945), *Pippi Goes On Board* (1946), *Do You Know Pippi Longstocking?* (1947), and *Pippi in the South Seas* (1948)—has been translated into more than sixty languages and published all over the world.

During the winter of 1941, Lindgren's seven-year-old daughter Karin was ill and asked her mother to tell her a story about Pippi Longstocking. The story Astrid Lindgren told delighted Karin and all her friends. A few years later, while recovering from an injury, Lindgren finally found the time to write down the Pippi stories. Lindgren's tenth birthday present to her daughter was the completed Pippi manuscript.

Lindgren submitted a revised version of the manuscript to the annual Rabén & Sjögren writing contest, where it won first prize. The book was published in December of 1945, and became an instant success. Rabén & Sjögren hired Lindgren as a children's book editor in 1946; she was soon put in charge of their children's book imprint, where she worked for many years. As one of the world's best loved writers, Astrid Lindgren has written more than seventy novels and storybooks, with over 145 million books sold worldwide.

Ingrid Vang Nyman (1916–1959) was a Danish-born

illustrator who was best known for her work on Swedish children's books. As a child, she suffered from tuberculosis, and at age thirteen, she lost vision in one eye.

Vang Nyman studied at the Royal Danish Academy of Fine Arts in Copenhagen before she moved to Stockholm, where her career in children's book illustration took off. She was briefly married to the poet and painter Arne Nyman, with whom she had a son named Peder. When the marriage ended in 1944, Ingrid Vang Nyman began a relationship with the lawyer and author Uno Eng. It was also around this time that she created the first images of Pippi Longstocking. Without a doubt, the feisty Pippi is somewhat of a kindred spirit with Vang Nyman, who had a strong faith in her own abilities—something not especially common among children's book illustrators of the day. Ingrid Vang Nyman went on to illustrate numerous children's books over the course of her brief career.

Tiina Nunnally is widely considered to be the preeminent translator

of Scandinavian languages into English. Her many awards and honors include the PEN/BOMC Translation Prize for her work on Sigrid Undset's *Kristin Lavransdatter*. She grew up in Milwaukee and received an M.A. in Scandinavian Studies from the University of Wisconsin.

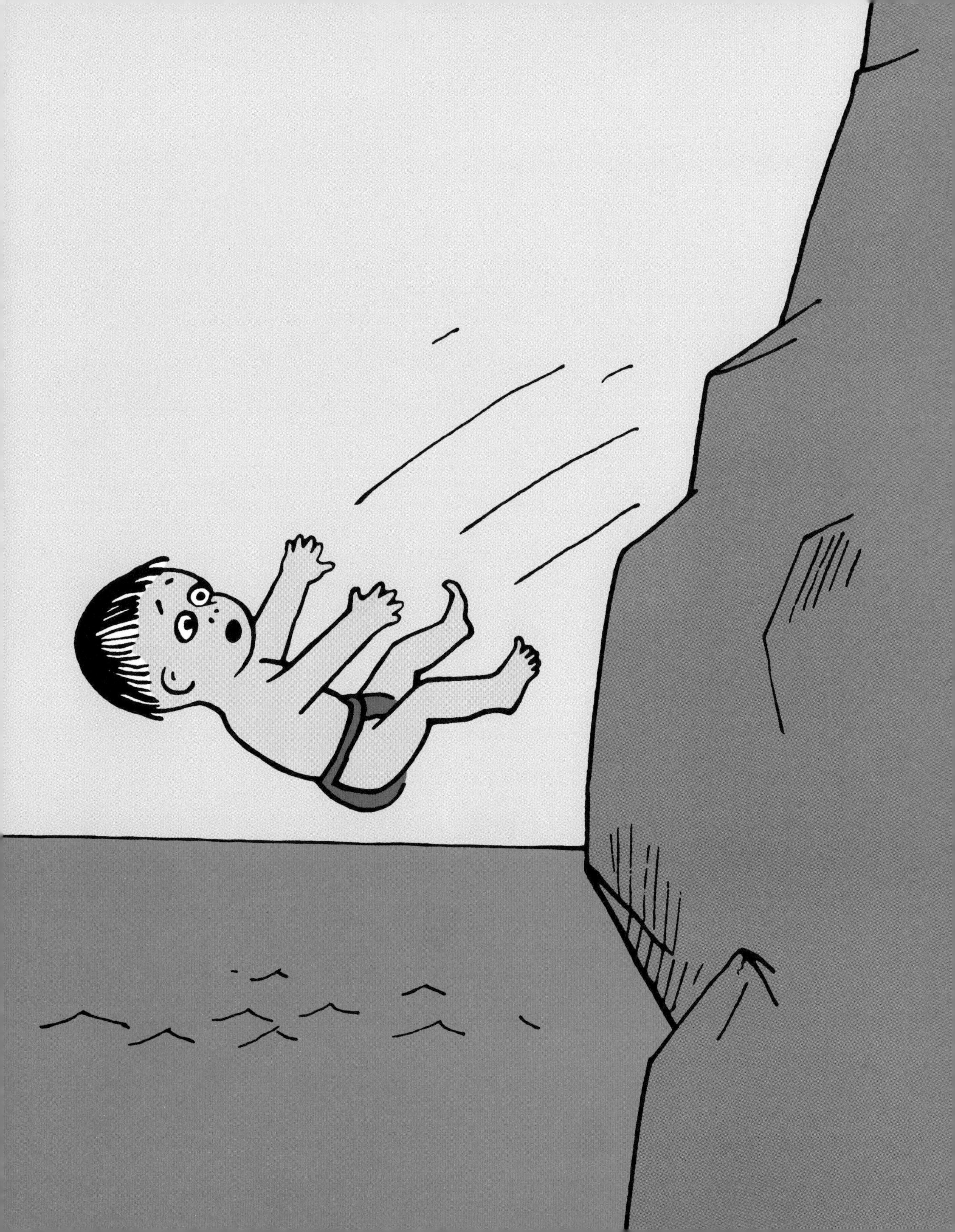

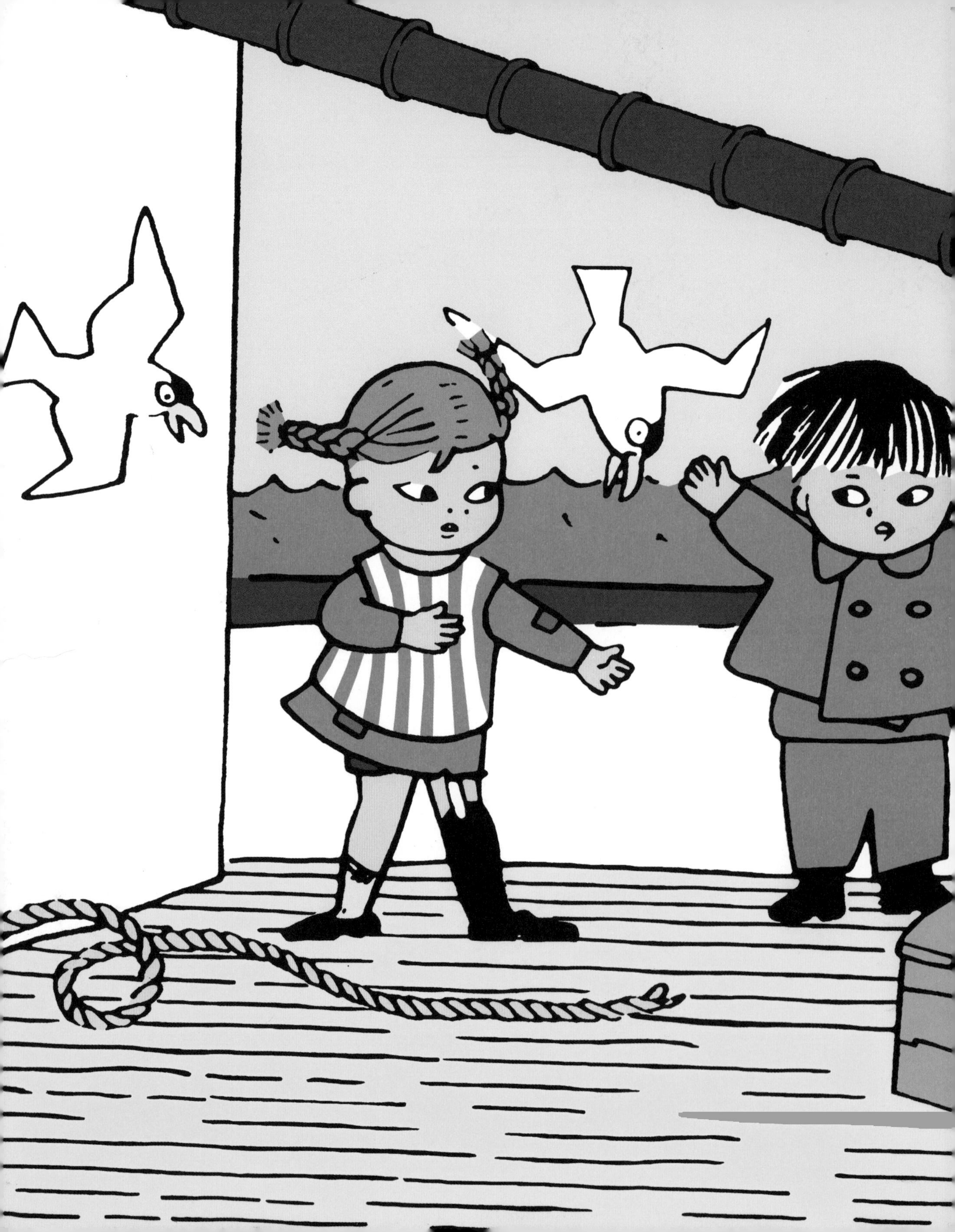

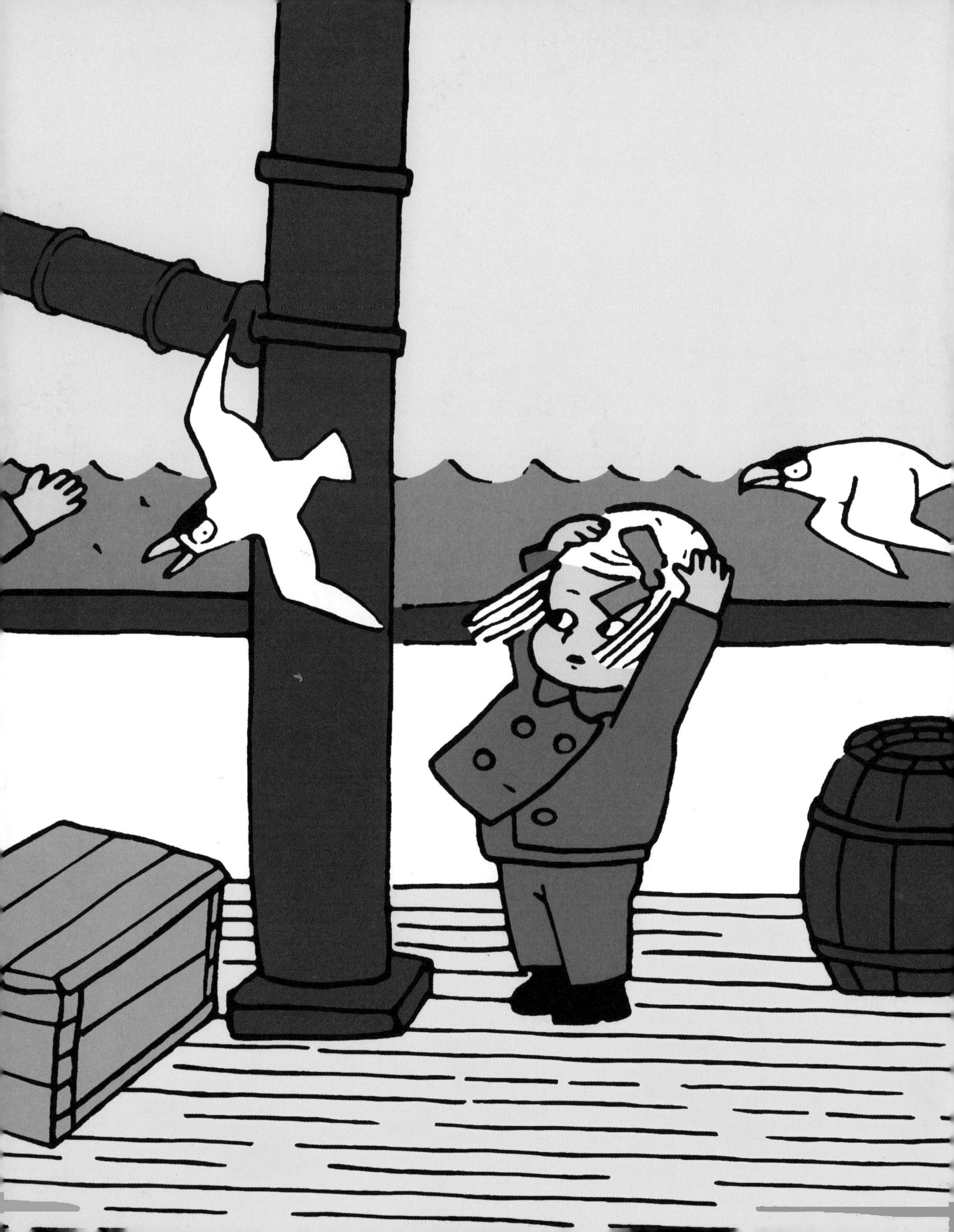

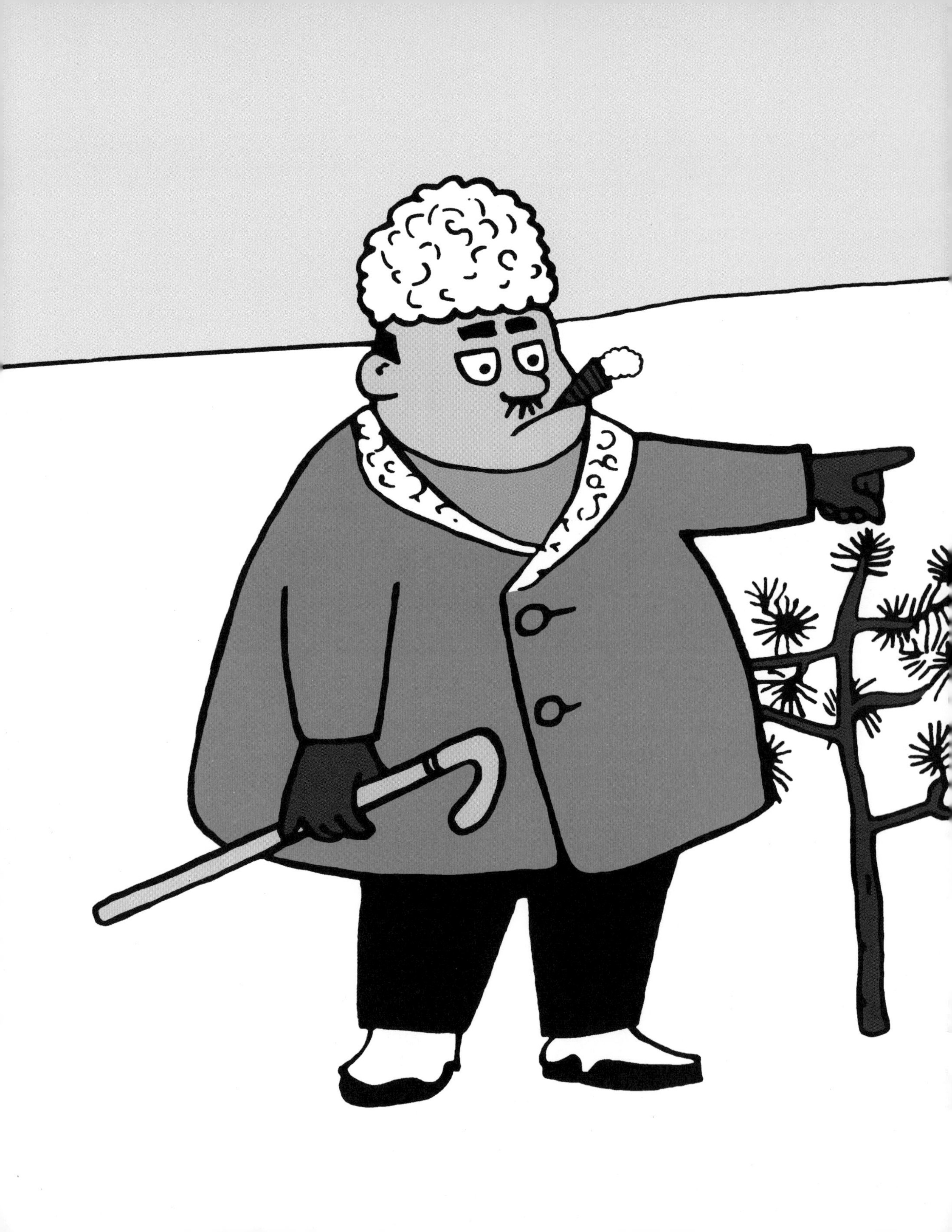

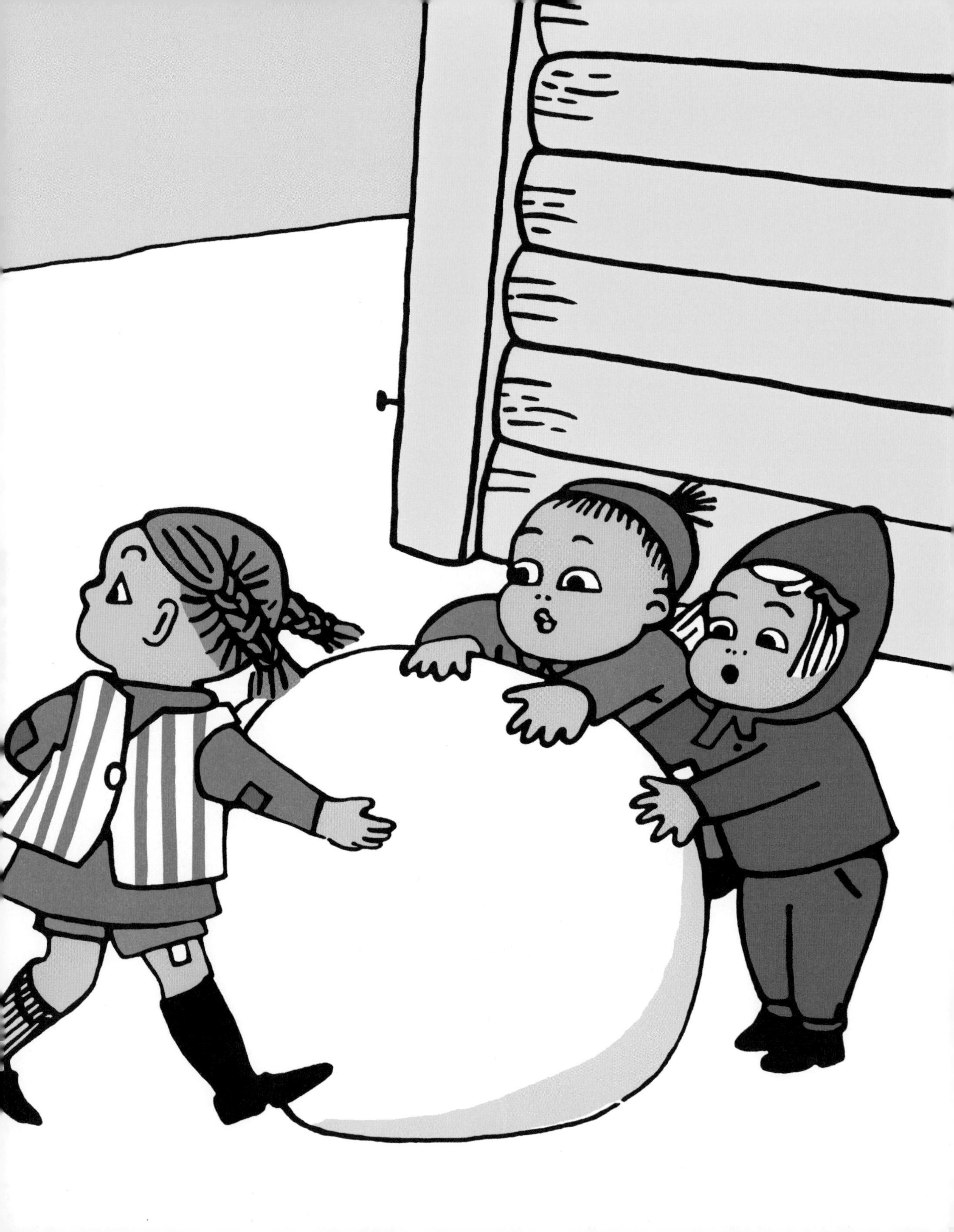

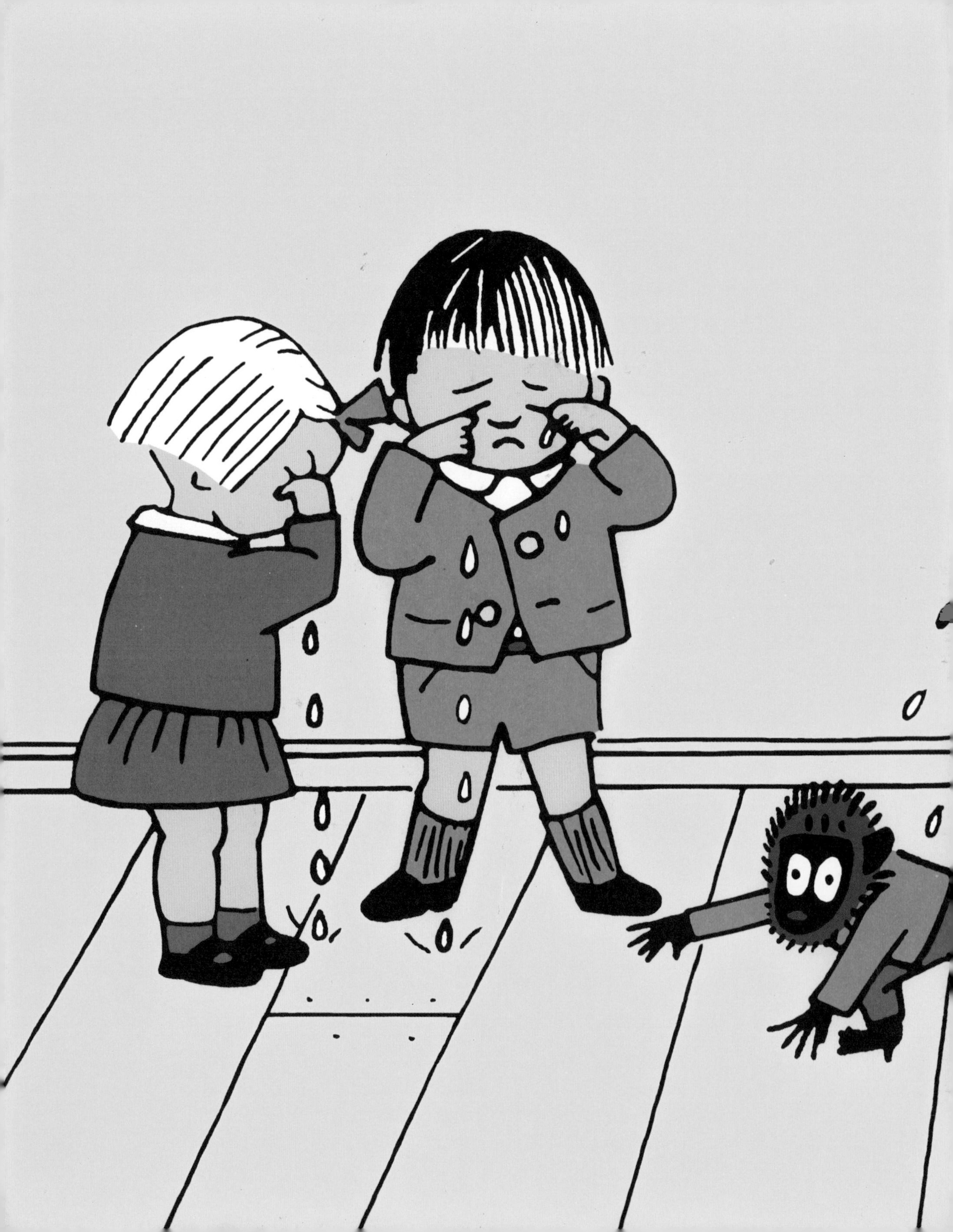